Human Rights

Human Rights

Look for these and other books in the Lucent Overview Series:

Abortion
Acid Rain
Adoption
Advertising
Alcoholism
Animal Rights
Artificial Organs
The Beginning of Writing
The Brain
Cancer
Censorship
Child Abuse
Children's Rights
Cities
The Collapse of the Soviet Union
Cults
Dealing with Death
Death Penalty
Democracy
Drug Abuse
Drugs and Sports
Drug Trafficking
Eating Disorders
Elections
Endangered Species
The End of Apartheid in South Africa
Energy Alternatives
Espionage
Ethnic Violence
Euthanasia
Extraterrestrial Life
Family Violence
Gangs
Garbage
Gay Rights
Genetic Engineering
The Greenhouse Effect
Gun Control
Hate Groups
Hazardous Waste
The Holocaust

Homeless Children
Homelessness
Illegal Immigration
Illiteracy
Immigration
Juvenile Crime
Memory
Mental Illness
Militias
Money
Ocean Pollution
Oil Spills
The Olympic Games
Organ Transplants
Ozone
The Palestinian-Israeli Accord
Pesticides
Police Brutality
Population
Poverty
Prisons
Rainforests
The Rebuilding of Bosnia
Recycling
The Reunification of Germany
Schools
Smoking
Space Exploration
Special Effects in the Movies
Sports in America
Suicide
The UFO Challenge
The United Nations
The U.S. Congress
The U.S. Presidency
Vanishing Wetlands
Vietnam
Women's Rights
World Hunger
Zoos

Human Rights

by Keith McGowan

LUCENT Overview Series

LUCENT BOOKS®

THOMSON
™
GALE

San Diego • Detroit • New York • San Francisco • Cleveland • New Haven, Conn. • Waterville, Maine • London • Munich

Acknowledgments are due Melinda Allman, Marcelo Coca, the librarians of the Minuteman Library Network (especially those at the Somerville and Newton libraries), Colleen Nicol, Lori Shein, and in particular Cora Landy, Vivian Wong, and Kelly Joyce.

LIBRARY OF CONGRESS CATALOGING-IN-PUBLICATION DATA

McGowan, Keith, 1968–
    Human rights / by Keith McGowan.
       p. cm. — (Lucent overview series)
Summary: An overview of human rights issues, including the historical basis for the movement to uphold human rights internationally, and a look at the state of civil, political, economic, and social rights today.
Includes bibliographical references and index.
    ISBN 1-56006-858-2 (hardback : alk. paper)
    1. Human Rights—Juvenile literature. [1. Human rights.] I. Title. II. Series.
    JC571 .M37 2003
    323—dc21

                                      2002005519

Contents

Introduction

THE TERM *HUMAN RIGHTS,* as it is used today, refers to a group of fundamental rights recognized by countries around the world. These rights were originally described more than fifty years ago in an international declaration called the Universal Declaration of Human Rights. They have since been detailed in a series of international agreements, called human rights agreements, similar to international treaties. Today, more than two-thirds of the countries in the world have pledged to uphold these rights.

Human rights include many things. Among them are the right to life, liberty, and personal security; the right not to be tortured or enslaved; the right to safe, decent work; and the right to an education. Whenever any of these rights is denied to an individual anywhere in the world, that individual's human rights are said to be violated. Thus, when black South Africans were denied the right to vote in their country, it was called a human rights violation. When women in Afghanistan were not allowed to go to school or to walk the streets without a male escort, it was called a human rights violation. And when workers today are forced to work sixteen-hour days for weeks on end with no rest sewing clothes in Bangladesh, it is called a human rights violation.

What unites these seemingly distinct events is that, in each instance, the people involved were denied their fundamental human rights as laid out by the Universal Declaration of Human Rights. In South Africa, the right denied to black South Africans was the right to participate in their government through free and fair elections. In Afghanistan, the rights denied to women were the right to an education and the right to move freely about their country. And in Bangladesh, the right denied to factory workers is the right to safe, decent working conditions.

"Achieving Global Justice"

Not every injustice in the world is a human rights violation. However, many injustices are. The vision expressed by those working against human rights abuses is one of humane treatment for all individuals, an end to poverty worldwide, and equality for women and men of all races, religions, and nationalities. "Realizing human rights," writes Princeton law professor Richard Falk, "is tantamount [equal] to achieving global justice."[1]

Few involved with the issue expect to achieve such a goal in their lifetimes. Nevertheless, the dream of such a future inspires individuals to protest human rights abuses whenever they occur and to work toward a day when people in every part of the world will enjoy basic human rights.

1

The Universal Declaration of Human Rights

On DECEMBER 10, 1948, a historic event occurred. Delegates from forty-eight nations representing all parts of the world came together to issue a declaration. In this declaration, called the Universal Declaration of Human Rights, these nations proclaimed that people everywhere had fundamental rights, called human rights. "All human beings are born free and equal in dignity and rights,"[2] the nations declared. They then described in detail the rights that all forty-eight nations agreed were fundamental rights, and each country pledged to uphold and promote these rights internationally.

The human rights recognized in this declaration were sweeping in scope. They included, among many others, the right to a fair, public trial if accused of a crime; the right to food, clothing, shelter, and medical care; the right to a free primary education; the right to participate in one's government, either directly or through elections; and the right to practice the religion of one's choice. So dramatic was the vision of rights set forth by these countries that one of the people who helped to draft the Universal Declaration of Human Rights, Charles Malik of Lebanon, later wrote: "the Declaration . . . was really something of a miracle."[3]

Malik called the declaration a miracle because, for the first time in history, countries from around the world had agreed on the rights they felt all women and men should have. Many countries already had constitutions that afforded rights to their citizens. The U.S. Constitution, for example, recognized a right to free speech, a right to a free press, and, according to a 1920 amendment, the right for women to vote. And the Swedish Constitution recognized, among other rights, the right to an education. The 1948 Universal Declaration of Human Rights was unique, though, because never before had so many countries come together to recognize *international* rights, those held by all people regardless of where they lived. Moreover, the rights recognized in the Universal Declaration went far beyond those recognized within most countries. Many people at the time were therefore surprised that so many countries, with such different histories, cultures, and laws, agreed on a declaration describing international support for a broad range of rights.

Nevertheless, the group of countries that signed the declaration did just that, and their Universal Declaration of Human Rights has since served as the starting point for a series of international agreements expanding on its vision. Today, more than two-thirds of the nations in the world are parties to these agreements, and all nations in the world are affected by them.

The Universal Declaration of Human Rights has "profoundly changed the international landscape,"[4] explains political scholar Johannes Morsink. The declaration has had a significant impact on world politics, war and peace, economics, and the lives of people all over the world. How the declaration came to be and the exact rights described within it are key parts of a history that continues to shape the world.

Ideals Born from the Devastation of World War II

To understand why so many countries agreed to the Universal Declaration of Human Rights, it is necessary to understand the state of mind of people in the world at the time the declaration was made. The declaration was written and signed in the late 1940s, just after World War II. Much of Europe and parts of Asia and Africa had been destroyed. Millions were dead.

Prisoners of a Nazi concentration camp. When the horrors of the Holocaust were exposed after World War II, human rights became an issue of international importance.

Moreover, the concentration camps established by the German Nazi government had shocked the conscience of humanity. These facilities operated as human slaughterhouses, where Jews, gypsies, homosexuals, prisoners of war, and others were shipped by train, unloaded, forced into cement rooms with the metal doors barricaded, and killed with poison gas. After death, the bodies were often stripped of the valuable gold from their teeth and sometimes shorn of their hair, which would be used to manufacture cloth sold to the public.

The horrors of these death camps, in addition to the destruction brought by the war itself, led many people to dream of a world that would be the opposite of the world at war—a world at peace, where all peoples would be treated with dignity. One young man, Kim Malthe-Bruun, who joined the Danish resistance against the Nazis, expressed this attitude in a letter written home before he was killed:

I want you all to remember that you must not dream yourselves back to the times before the war, but the dream for you all, young and old, must be to create an ideal of human decency, and not a narrow-minded and prejudiced one. That is the great gift our country hungers for, something every little peasant boy can look forward to, and with pleasure feel he is a part of—something he can work and fight for.[5]

The words *human rights* were often used when people described the kind of future Malthe-Bruun envisioned. A future based on an ideal of human decency was one where all people would hold certain fundamental human rights, many people said. Never again should individuals be left to suffer enslavement, torture, and death under a government plan such as that of the Nazi concentration camps, no matter what country they lived in or who they were. All people, it was asserted, must be recognized to have certain basic rights.

The Four Freedoms

World leaders, including U.S. president Franklin Roosevelt and British prime minister Winston Churchill, regularly used the words *human rights* when they described their vision of the world after the war. Roosevelt, in particular, gave a speech that would later become famous for such language. In this speech, Roosevelt described four freedoms that he believed should be recognized worldwide, and he connected these freedoms to the term *human rights*. Roosevelt said in 1941:

In the future days . . . we look forward to a world founded upon four essential human freedoms. The first is freedom of speech and expression. . . . The second is freedom of every person to worship God in his own way. . . . The third is freedom from want. . . . The fourth is freedom from fear, which, translated into world terms, means a world-wide reduction of armaments to such a point . . . that no nation will be in a position to commit an act of physical aggression against any neighbor. . . . This is no vision of a distant millennium. It is a definite basis for a kind of world attainable in our own time and generation.

Roosevelt proclaimed that respect for these four freedoms would mean "the supremacy of human rights everywhere."[6]

Roosevelt's call for all nations to recognize and respect these four freedoms—and therefore human rights—was embraced as part of a broad international rights movement during that time. This movement, promoted by international organizations, religious groups, and ordinary people in different parts of the world, maintained that recognition of human rights worldwide had to be a central part of any World War II peace settlement.

The United Nations

In the late spring and early summer of 1945, as World War II drew to a close, the shape of the new peace came into clearer focus. Representatives from fifty countries met in San Francisco, California, and agreed to join together into a new international organization called the United Nations (UN). The UN was initially conceived as an organization to keep peace and guarantee security worldwide, not as an instrument to further fundamental human rights for the peoples of the world. But, as Harvard law professor Mary Ann Glendon explains: "When delegates began to arrive in San Francisco from fifty far-flung lands in April 1945, they included a number of individuals who hoped that the new organization would concern itself with much more than collective security."[7] These delegates wanted the countries in the UN to pledge to promote not only security but also human rights everywhere. Representatives from Canada to India to the Philippines and elsewhere all argued that the new UN should proclaim respect for universal human rights. In addition, religious groups, labor organizations, and legal groups also lobbied at these early meetings for a firm commitment to promote and protect human rights. Respect for human rights, these organizations maintained, would help preserve the peace in the long term.

"To Reaffirm Our Faith in Fundamental Human Rights"

The push by these delegates and organizations to declare human rights central to international peace was ultimately successful. On June 26, 1945, the fifty countries of the newly formed UN signed the UN Charter, which put forth the aims of the UN and included a clear and forthright commitment to human rights. The charter stated in its preamble that the countries of the UN were determined "to save succeeding generations from the scourge of war . . . [and] to reaffirm our faith in fundamental human rights, in the dignity and worth of the human person."[8]

The countries of the UN thus pledged themselves, that summer in 1945, not only to promote peace but also to promote respect for human rights everywhere in the world. For many of the representatives, these two concepts were inextricably linked. A world where all people were allowed to live in dignity was believed to be the only world where peace could prevail.

On August 6, 1945, just six weeks after the UN Charter was signed, U.S. president Harry Truman authorized the use of the atomic bomb against Japan. The use of the atomic

Leaders of many countries gather in San Francisco, CA, at the first meeting of the United Nations.

bomb highlighted the need for peace and the simultaneous need for worldwide respect of human rights. Without respect for human rights, many people involved in politics believed, peace would never last. Former First Lady Eleanor Roosevelt later wrote: "We came into a new world [after the development and use of the atomic bomb]—a world in which we had to learn to live in friendship with our neighbors of every race and creed and color, or face the fact that we might be wiped off the face of the earth."[9]

The UN Human Rights Commission

The countries of the UN declared in 1945 their commitment to human rights and fundamental freedoms, but two basic questions still needed answering: What were these human rights and fundamental freedoms exactly, and how would countries assure these rights and freedoms were respected? The UN assigned the members of its Economic and Social Council the task of answering these difficult questions. The Economic and Social Council decided to create a small UN Human Rights Commission to undertake the duty.

Representatives from eighteen countries were placed on the first Human Rights Commission. These countries were Australia, Belgium, Byelorussia, Chile, China, Egypt, France, India, Iran, Lebanon, Panama, the Philippines, the Ukraine, the U.S.S.R., the United Kingdom, the United States, Uruguay, and Yugoslavia. The U.S. representative, Eleanor Roosevelt, was elected by the other commission members to serve as chair. Peng-chun (P.C.) Chang of China was elected vice chairman, and Charles Malik of Lebanon was named rapporteur, or secretary, responsible for preparing the commission's official reports. A Canadian, John Humphreys, became the secretariat to the commission. Humphreys represented no country; rather he served as a UN employee whose job it was to aid the commission members in their duties.

For more than a year, the Human Rights Commission met many times, usually on Long Island, New York, arguing and debating occasionally late into the night. One of the commission's central objectives was to draft a document that would describe in detail the human rights that all countries in the UN

might agree were fundamental human rights. This was a formidable task. To accomplish it, members of the commission consulted the constitutions and laws of countries around the world to see what rights each country afforded its own citizens. Commission members also looked at political writings throughout history and received reports from a separate group set up by the UN to look into how an international human rights document might fit in with the world's many religious and philosophical traditions. After each step, the eighteen representatives on the Human Rights Commission, either together or in smaller groups, argued and debated some more.

Eleanor Roosevelt (center) and other members of the UN Human Rights Commission meet in New York City in 1946.

The Universal Declaration of Human Rights

A year and a half after their first meeting, the commission members finally completed a draft of the document that would ultimately be called the Universal Declaration of Human Rights. The document included all of the rights that the commission believed the UN should accept as universal human rights. Then, in the fall of 1948, the commission brought that draft document before representatives of the member countries of the UN. By that time, the UN included fifty-six nations.

Debate started all over again that fall, with many UN representatives arguing over points that the commission had debated long before. A letter written by UN secretariat John Humphreys to his sister during one of those sessions shows the mood of the commission members at that time:

One of the first documents published by the UN, the Universal Declaration of Human Rights, took more than a year to create.

I am writing this letter during a session of the Third Committee of the [UN] General Assembly. I suppose I should be listening to the South American gentleman who is expounding on Article 3 of the Declaration of Human Rights, but I have heard so many of these speeches that it is only in revolt that I can hope to find sanity. We have been on this thing for 3 weeks now and have adopted 2 out of 28 articles. When we will finish the Lord only knows. [10]

Despite the endless debates, however, Humphreys and others still had hopes that the declaration would ultimately be adopted by the UN. After he finished expressing his frustrations in the letter, Humphreys wrote: "But I am really very happy about the way things have gone so far and fully expect that the General Assembly will adopt the declaration substantially as it was drafted by the Human Rights Commission."[11]

Humphreys was correct in his expectation. The Universal Declaration of Human Rights was adopted by the UN General Assembly on December 10, 1948. Forty-eight countries voted in favor of the declaration and eight countries abstained. The abstaining countries were Byelorussia, Czechoslovakia, Poland, Saudi Arabia, South Africa, the Ukraine, the U.S.S.R., and Yugoslavia. No country voted against the declaration. Thus, the push that began during World War II for international recognition of fundamental rights and freedoms finally succeeded in the winter of 1948.

"The Foundation of Freedom, Justice, and Peace in the World"

The declaration was a well-crafted and carefully conceived document. It included a preamble explaining the reasons such an international declaration was believed to be necessary, followed by twenty-seven articles, brief sections describing the human rights that most of the countries of the UN were able to agree upon. Finally, the last three articles of the declaration, Articles 28 through 30, stressed the duties and responsibilities that went with those rights.

The declaration's preamble began the document by describing the reasons the countries of the UN had decided to recognize international human rights. "[R]ecognition of the inherent dignity and of the equal and inalienable rights of all members of the human family is the foundation of freedom, justice, and peace in the world," it stated, and "disregard and contempt for human rights have resulted in barbarous acts which have outraged the conscience of mankind." The preamble also made specific reference to U.S. president Roosevelt's 1941 four freedoms speech, stating that "the advent [coming into being] of a world in which human beings shall enjoy freedom of speech and belief and freedom from fear and want has been proclaimed as the highest aspiration of the common people."[12]

The preamble was followed by the declaration's first two articles. These emphasized, among other things, the central ideal of the declaration: equality of rights worldwide. The declaration was, after all, a "universal declaration," written to put forward the rights of all people—women and men, people of all religions, and people of all races and nationalities. The second article of the declaration, Article 2, stated this ideal of equality in plain terms. "Everyone is entitled to all the rights and freedoms set forth in this Declaration," it read, "without distinction of any kind, such as race, colour, sex, language, religion, political or other opinion, national or social origin, property, birth or other status."[13]

Civil and Political Rights

The next group of articles, Articles 3 through 21, described rights generally known as "civil and political rights." Many of these were inspired by rights first described in the seventeenth century by Western philosophers. They included the right to life, liberty, and personal security and the right to live free from cruel, inhuman treatment. They also included rights to free speech, free assembly, a free press, and freedom of religion. Civil and political rights further encompassed legal rights, including the right to a fair, public hearing if accused of a crime and the right to be presumed innocent before the law until proven guilty.

Most of these civil and political rights are found in constitutions written during the eighteenth century, including the U.S. and French constitutions. However, in the Universal Declaration of Human Rights, the countries of the UN expanded on and adapted these rights to fit modern times; the declaration stated, for example, that "slavery and the slave trade shall be prohibited in all their forms."[14] Moreover, with the atrocities of World War II in mind, the drafters of the declaration also made sure to include the rights not to be tortured or "subjected to arbitrary arrest, detention or exile."[15] Further, because so many people fleeing Germany to escape the concentration camps had been turned away by other countries, the declaration included the right "to seek and enjoy in other countries asylum from persecution" [16] as a civil and political human right.

Economic and Social Rights

Articles 22 through 27 of the Universal Declaration described rights known as "economic and social rights." These were rights that had generally been recognized by countries since the rise of the industrial era in the 1800s. They included the right to food, clothing, shelter, and medical care; the right to safe working conditions; the right to social assistance if one could not find work; and the right to an education.

Economic and social rights were inspired in part by the poor working conditions that many people faced in the industrial age. During the nineteenth and early twentieth centuries, women, men, and children labored long hours for little pay in the factories and mines that built the modern world. Economic and social rights were also influenced by an economic depression in the 1930s; during this time people in many countries could not find work and were driven into extreme poverty. The devastation of World War II only added to this poverty, since countless towns and cities worldwide were destroyed.

These conditions led Eleanor Roosevelt, among others, to note after the war that "freedom without bread . . . has little meaning." [17] With this statement, Roosevelt expressed an opinion that was common among the representatives of UN countries. Civil and political rights to free speech, equality before the law, and other related freedoms meant little, they felt, if a person did not also have the right to food, clothing, shelter, and work. For this reason, the UN representatives made sure to include economic and social rights as part of an individual's basic human rights.

Duties and Responsibilities

The final three articles of the Universal Declaration of Human Rights did not describe rights. Rather they stressed the idea that an individual's human rights could be upheld only if all others in society agreed to take on certain duties and responsibilities. Every right in the declaration placed a responsibility on society. Respect for one person's right to freedom

Among the many economic and social rights guaranteed by the Universal Declaration was the right to an education.

of religion, for example, meant that others needed to refrain from actions that interfered with that person's religious practices. Respect for one person's right to a fair hearing when accused of a crime, meanwhile, meant that others needed to create and support a judicial system to assure such a hearing. The right not to be tortured placed a responsibility on people not to torture others. And the right to an education placed a responsibility on society and governments to provide an education for all people.

The UN delegates who drafted the declaration recognized this fact. They included references to the duties and responsibilities of society primarily in two places within the declaration: Article 28 and Article 1. Article 28 stated: "Everyone is entitled to a social and international order in which the rights and freedoms set forth in this Declaration can be fully realized."[18] And Article 1 stated in part that all human beings "are endowed with reason and conscience and should act towards one another in a spirit of brotherhood."[19] These two statements were meant to be understood as a recognition that all of the rights described in the declaration necessarily placed duties and responsibilities on society. The countries that signed the declaration therefore recognized not only the rights of individuals; they also recognized that, if these rights were to be upheld, all people in the world had responsibilities to each other.

Beyond a Declaration of Rights

Writing the Universal Declaration of Human Rights and working to convince the countries of the UN to adopt that document was a significant accomplishment for the Human Rights Commission. To this day, the declaration remains the most important human rights document in the world. Mary Robinson, the UN High Commissioner for Human Rights, explains:

> The Universal Declaration is not just another international document. It is the primary proclamation of the international community's commitment to human rights as "a common standard of achievement for all peoples and all nations." Its message is one of hope, equality, liberation, and empowerment. It is a message to all who are committed to freedom, justice, and peace in the world.[20]

The declaration, however, did not answer one important question that had been posed to the Human Rights Commission, namely, how human rights were going to be protected. The Universal Declaration of Human Rights itself was not a legally binding document. The forty-eight countries that signed it agreed to work toward a future where human rights would be respected. But they did not agree that, if they did not uphold the human rights of their citizens, they could be made to answer for violating the declaration.

Many of the representatives on the UN Human Rights Commission, even as the Universal Declaration was being written, were concerned about this point. They argued that the commission should write a stronger international document on human rights, one called a covenant, an agreement that would be legally binding. Representatives from Australia, Belgium, China, France, and India, among others, were in favor of drafting a stronger, legally binding covenant.

The covenant proposed by these countries would not only describe the rights that all of the UN nations agreed were universally held by people everywhere, it would also include a legally binding pledge to uphold these rights and describe a way to enforce that pledge. The Australian representative Colonel William Roy Hodgson envisioned an international court, for example, where people could bring grievances against their governments if their human rights were being violated.

Because of the desire by some of the commission members for a document stronger than the simple declaration, the Human Rights Commission also worked on a version of a human rights covenant even as the Universal Declaration of Human Rights was being written. Ultimately, however, the legally binding covenant proved too controversial for its time. Most of the countries in the UN could agree to sign the nonbinding declaration, pledging to work toward a time when the rights described in the declaration would be upheld. But they could not be convinced to sign a covenant that would legally bind them to uphold these rights and would sanction them if they did not. For this reason, the covenant was blocked by the representatives of some countries, including those from the United States and the U.S.S.R. The declaration was therefore finished and accepted by the UN General Assembly, and the covenant was temporarily put aside.

Human Rights Agreements of Later Years

Many years later, however, with more political support behind the idea, legally binding human rights covenants were finally completed, brought before the UN General Assembly, and adopted. In 1966, the International Covenant on Economic, Social, and Cultural Rights and the International Covenant on Civil and Political Rights were both adopted by the UN General Assembly. In 1979, the Convention on the Elimination of All Forms of Discrimination Against Women was adopted by the UN, and in 1989 the UN further adopted a Convention on the Rights of the Child. Each of these documents reiterated and expanded upon the pledges made in the Universal Declaration of Human Rights.

By signing onto these expanded agreements, countries voluntarily strengthened their pledges to uphold the human rights described within each. Each of these international human rights agreements has been ratified today by more than 135 countries—more than two-thirds of the nations in the world. All of these international agreements were inspired by and make reference to the original 1948 Universal Declaration of Human Rights.

Today, people all over the world are not only guaranteed rights through their national constitutions and national laws, they are also guaranteed rights through a system of international human rights agreements. The first of these agreements, the Universal Declaration, stands as the central pillar of this international framework. The declaration is the primary expression of an international vision for a world of peace, a world where women and men in every part of the world have fundamental rights.

2

Government Brutality

ON SEPTEMBER 11, 1973, General Augusto Pinochet led the Chilean armed forces on an attack against Chile's democratically elected president, Salvador Allende, and bombed the presidential palace *La Moneda*—Chile's equivalent of the White House—with military jets. General Pinochet's goal was to take over the country.

Two hours before the bombs began to fall, Chile's president Allende, aware of the coup, broadcast a speech to the nation over the radio. To this day, many Chileans remember listening to that speech from their homes or workplaces. President Allende vowed that he would not yield to the military coup. "I will pay with my life [for] the loyalty of the people,"[21] he told the citizens of Chile. Editor and journalist Marc Cooper, who worked as a translator at *La Moneda* at the time, explains what happened next: "Within hours, the Moneda was rocketed and burned . . . Allende was dead, [the Chilean] Congress was padlocked . . . and Gen. Augusto Pinochet was in power."[22]

General Pinochet and the other military leaders involved in the coup immediately took action to secure control of the previously democratic country. In the days and weeks that followed, Pinochet and his coconspirators attempted to have anyone they thought might oppose them arrested or killed. Author Arturo Valenzuela and journalist Pamela Constable explain: "By December, at least fifteen hundred civilians were dead—shot in confrontations, tortured to death, hunted down by vigilantes, or executed by firing squads."[23] Thousands more were imprisoned. Many were arrested in secret, taken from their homes late at night to be held in secret detention centers where they were tortured or murdered. Men and women in Chile's capital city, Santiago, and elsewhere simply disappeared, never to be heard from again. These people became known as "the disappeared"—*desaparecidos* in Spanish. A journalist who lived in Santiago in October 1973 described the situation: "Dozens of women would station themselves at the bridges [over the Mapocho River in Santiago] every day, in hopes of seeing the body of a husband or son who had disappeared after being picked up by the soldiers." Bodies often floated down the river, presumably thrown in after execution. The journalist continued: "One day I saw nine corpses, all with bare chests, hands tied behind their backs. The bodies were perforated by bullet holes. And with them was the body of a girl, apparently fifteen or sixteen years old."[24]

Smoke billows from La Moneda, the Chilean presidential palace, during General Pinochet's 1973 coup.

Violating Human Rights

Pinochet's government in Chile stands as an example of a government that brutalized its citizens—imprisoning, torturing, and executing them at will. This type of government brutality has long been decried by people of all cultures and religions and, today, is formally condemned by the Universal Declaration and by a series of international human rights agreements. These agreements include the 1966 International Covenant on Civil and Political Rights and the 1984 Convention Against Torture and Other Cruel, Inhuman or Degrading Treatment or Punishment.

Despite such condemnation, government brutality has been common around the globe in recent decades. From the Central American country of Guatemala to the Southeast Asian country of Cambodia, governments have used fear, intimidation, and violence to control their citizens. These governments have used tactics, including torture, arbitrary imprisonment, and even genocide, to maintain their own political and military power. Whenever these tactics are used—whether by government officials, soldiers at war, or police officers—such acts are violations of citizens' human rights.

Torture

It may seem to people living quiet lives in relatively peaceful parts of the world that such brutal tactics are rare. However, a look at statistics and reports on such acts reveals otherwise. Considering the use of torture alone, the human rights organization Amnesty International reported in 2000 that acts of torture occurred in approximately 125 countries and were widespread and persistent in more than 70 countries.

The most common form of torture, Amnesty reported, was beating. Other common techniques include rape and sexual assault, electric shocks, and hanging a person in the air by ropes or cords. Torture also typically includes psychological trauma. It can involve sensory deprivation—where a person's head is covered by a sack for days on end, for example, blinding and disorienting the person. Or it may include months of solitary confinement. The simple act of waiting to be tortured can also be devastating. Author John Conroy, who has studied the effects of torture, notes: "When survivors [of torture] were asked to indicate what they thought was the worst part of their detention, they often cited the periods between torture sessions, when they were frightened of what was going to happen."[25]

Even the briefest glance at accounts of torture illustrates the brutality it entails. Dianna Ortiz, for example, an American nun who was tortured by military officials in Guatemala, recalled her experience in a 2000 interview. "They [the military officials] left me in a dark cell, where I listened to the cries of a man and woman being tortured," Ortiz explained. "When the men returned, they accused me of being a guerrilla and began interrogating me. For every answer I gave them, they burned my back or my chest with cigarettes. Afterwards, they gang-raped me." Ortiz was then placed in a cell with another woman and forced to share in the woman's murder—a form of psychological torture. She said:

> The policeman put a machete into my hands. Thinking it would be used against me, and at that point in my torture wanting to die, I did not resist. But the policeman put his hands onto the handle, on top of mine, and forced me to stab [the other] woman [in the room] again and again. What I remember is blood gushing—spurting like a water fountain—droplets of blood spattering everywhere—and my cries lost in the cries of the woman. [26]

Torture Is Used to Stop Political Opposition

Governments often use torture to further their political ends—to hold on to power, to intimidate or punish people who form opposition political parties, or to silence those who criticize the government. Torture has been used for such purposes, for example, from the late 1990s through the year 2002 in the former Soviet republic of Uzbekistan in Central Asia. The current president of that country, Islam Karimov, a former Soviet boss, is concerned with a movement that seeks to replace his government with one based on Islamic law. As

American nun Dianna Ortiz shows composite drawings of her attackers. Ortiz was a victim of military torture in Guatemala.

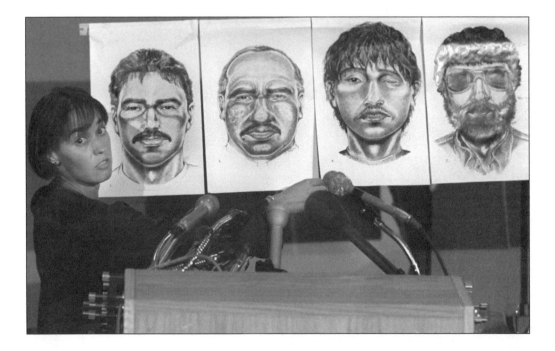

part of a government crackdown designed to stop this movement, Karimov has overseen the arrest of thousands of peaceful Muslims. Many of those arrested have reportedly done nothing more than pray at mosques that the government believes are associated with the political movement against it. Once arrested, many people have been tortured to confess to crimes that they did not commit and then jailed. Some Uzbeks have died as a result of the torture.

The current government of Uzbekistan is only one of many governments in recent years to use torture to try to crush political opposition or silence government critics. From the 1970s to the present, such acts have been perpetrated by governments in Argentina, Burkina Faso, Cambodia, Chad, Honduras, Morocco, Peru, and Turkey, among many other countries.

Torture and Western Democracies

Torture is sometimes portrayed as a method used only by dictators, authoritarian governments, or unstable governments struggling to keep power in the poorer countries of the world. However, such a portrayal is not accurate. Western democracies have also been known to promote the use of torture when it is politically useful. In fact, many democracies have been embroiled in controversies over torture in the years since World War II.

In Britain, for example, the use of torture by government officials became an issue in the 1970s. During that decade, British security officers reportedly tortured Irish prisoners. The torture of these men occurred as part of Britain's attempt to keep control of the disputed region known as Northern Ireland. Irish prisoners were made to stand for days on end spread-eagle, with their hands against a wall, without being allowed to sleep. A hood was placed over their heads so they could not see, and a loud motorized noise around them was maintained so they could not hear. During this time, they were also deprived of food and water and occasionally beaten. The effect of such treatment was devastating to the prisoners. Says author John Conroy, "In combination, they [the torture techniques] induced a state of psychosis, a temporary madness with long-lasting aftereffects."[27]

More recently, in the mid-1990s, the U.S. government also became embroiled in a controversy over torture when it was revealed that the U.S. Army was training Latin American military officers in techniques of torture at a military training school in Fort Benning, Georgia. At the time, the U.S. government supported several regimes in Latin America that used torture on their citizens to quell political opposition. Officers were brought to the school from these and other Latin American countries to receive military training—including training in "torture, extortion, censorship, false arrest, execution and the 'neutralizing' of enemies,"[28] reported the *New York Times*. When the details of the training were revealed to the American public, human rights groups and U.S. congressmen protested what they called government-sponsored promotion of torture. The protests were successful, and the military training classes were subsequently changed to exclude all instruction in such techniques.

The use of torture is therefore an international issue, one which over the years has involved governments all over the world, from dictatorships in impoverished nations to democratically elected governments in the West. "The phenomenon of torture continues to plague all regions of the world,"[29] the UN Special Rapporteur, or special reporter, on torture, concluded in October 1999.

Prisoners of Conscience

Torture is just one of the brutal techniques that modern governments use to further their political goals. Many governments also use their prison systems as a way to silence critics or to halt movements within their countries that the governments find threatening. Today, governments all over the world put people in jail for speaking out against government policies, for publishing newspaper articles that criticize the government, for gathering in peaceful assemblies to protest government policies, or even just for being a member of a certain ethnic or religious group that the government finds threatening.

When people are jailed for any of these reasons, they are generally called political prisoners or prisoners of conscience. The detention of prisoners of conscience violates many of the rights described in international human rights agreements.

Some of the human rights that may be violated when a prisoner of conscience is held by a government include the right not to be arbitrarily arrested; the right to a fair, public trial; the right to freedom of speech, freedom of assembly, and freedom of association; the right to impart information through the media; and the right to practice one's religion.

Today, prisoners of conscience are being held in approximately sixty countries. Some of these prisoners are held for only a few days. For example, in March 2002 in the western African country of Liberia, members of a human rights group called the National Human Rights Center of Liberia were arrested and held for several days after criticizing the government in a press release. Other prisoners of conscience, however, are held for a significant portion of their lives. This happened to Tibetan primary-school teacher Jigme Sangpo, who was arrested in China in 1983 for "spreading counter-revolutionary propaganda,"[30] according to the human rights group Amnesty International, after hanging a wall poster calling for Tibetan independence. (Tibet is a disputed region of

A Tibetan youth protests against Chinese control of his country.

China that has been under the control of the Chinese government since 1951.) Sangpo's prison sentence was extended twice for continuing to express opinions in favor of Tibetan independence while in prison. He ultimately spent more than nineteen years of his life in prison before he was released in April 2002 at the age of seventy-six.

Number of Prisoners Held and Prison Conditions Vary

The number of prisoners of conscience that each country holds varies. Some countries hold only a handful of prisoners of conscience in their jails, while others hold hundreds or even thousands of prisoners of conscience. The latter is the case in the Southeast Asian country of Myanmar, also known as Burma, which is ruled by a military dictatorship. More than a thousand prisoners of conscience arc currently detained in this country. Many of these prisoners of conscience are members of the National League for Democracy, a political party that won more than 80 percent of the seats in a democratic election in that country in 1990. The military regime has imprisoned these people as part of the regime's efforts to maintain power after the election.

The conditions in which prisoners of conscience live also vary from country to country. One prisoner of conscience may be held in relatively decent jail conditions, while another may be held in a squalid and dangerous prison. In Myanmar, for example, Aung San Suu Kyi, the head of the National League for Democracy and winner of the 1991 Nobel Peace Prize, was held from 1989 to 1995 and again from 2000 to 2002 under house arrest—imprisoned and unable to assume her role as democratically elected leader of that country, but nevertheless allowed to live in her own house in decent conditions. On the other hand, Freedom Neruda, a journalist, in Côte d'Ivoire, a country in western Africa, was jailed in the 1990s for criticizing his government and was held in extremely harsh conditions in a jail called Naca Prison. Neruda described his time in prison in a 2000 interview: "Naca Prison is a very hard one. It is the biggest prison in the Ivory Coast [Côte d'Ivoire]. There were six thousand inmates when we arrived and over one hundred died in detention during the first four months of 1996. We were so poor that we could never get enough to eat and constant vomiting reduced people to skeletons."[31] Typically, prisoners of conscience are held in regular jails within their countries and therefore live in the same conditions as prisoners who are arrested for nonpolitical crimes.

Genocide

Government brutality has occasionally gone beyond torture and politically motivated imprisonment—both relatively common human rights violations—to embrace a policy called genocide. In the case of genocide, a government attempts to slaughter part or all of a certain race, ethnicity, nationality, or religion. The term *genocide* was coined by Jewish linguist Raphael Lemkin during World War II to describe Nazi Germany's policy of killing all the Jews in Europe. Genocide is often called a crime against humanity, and it is literally a crime under international law, "condemned by the civilized world."[32] This is according to the UN Convention on the Prevention and Punishment of the Crime of Genocide, an international agreement adopted by the UN on December 9, 1948.

One recent example of genocide occurred in 1994 in the central African country of Rwanda. After the president of Rwanda, Juvenal Habyarimana, was killed on April 6 of that year—his plane shot down as it tried to land in the Rwandan capital of Kigali—violent members of the country's majority ethnic group, called Hutus, took over and launched a campaign to systematically slaughter all Rwandans belonging to the Tutsi ethnic group, a minority in the country. The slaughter also extended to any Hutus who sympathized with or protected Tutsis.

Between April and July 1994, approximately 800,000 to 850,000 Tutsis were massacred—an average of 8,000 every day. Since the plan was to kill all Tutsis so that none would exist within the country, even children and infants were murdered. Journalist Gerard Prunier describes the Rwandan genocide:

The killings were not in any way clean or surgical. The use of machetes often resulted in a long and painful agony and many people, when they had some money, paid their killers to be finished off quickly with a bullet rather than being slowly hacked to death. . . . Sexual abuse of women was common and they were often brutally killed after being raped . . . babies were often smashed against a rock or thrown alive into pit latrines.[33]

The genocide in Rwanda is only one of several genocides that have occurred in recent decades. According to scholars at Yale University, genocides also occurred in Cambodia in the 1970s and in East Timor and Yugoslavia in the 1990s.

"The Least We Can Do"

Dead refugees, victims of genocide, line a road in Rwanda in 1994.

Since the late 1940s, governments have pledged to prevent torture, arbitrary imprisonment, genocide, and other brutal government tactics. Despite these pledges, however, acts of government brutality continue to occur around the world. In

2000, the UN High Commissioner for Human Rights, Mary Robinson, noted:

> The last decade of the twentieth century witnessed one of the worst crimes in human history: the genocide in Rwanda. . . . The international community let down the people of Rwanda. The least we can do to honour the memory of the victims and to do justice to the survivors and their families is to redouble our resolve that such horrors will never be allowed to happen again.[34]

3

The Rights of People at Work

ZENAYDA TORRES IS one of millions of people who have been denied their economic human rights. In 1995, when she was nineteen years old, she went to work in a clothes-making factory outside of the Central American city of Managua, Nicaragua. She later recalled:

> The working conditions there were very hard. We worked from 7 am until 7 or 9 at night. Sometimes, when there was an urgent order, they made us work 24 hours straight. We worked weekends, often with no rest day. . . . Often, they wouldn't give you permission to go to the bathroom when you had to go; they would only let you go two or at most three times a day. [35]

Although she worked long hours under these difficult conditions, Torres was barely able to make enough money to live. She explained:

> We have a base wage of $65 a month, or 30 cents an hour . . . working a lot of overtime hours, it is possible to earn up to 45 cents an hour. . . . You can't live on that wage. It's not enough to buy the necessary food, clothing, medicine, transportation and household expenses. . . . Most workers and their families are living in real misery, in tiny houses with dirt floors. [36]

Torres and her coworkers, mostly young women, have little chance of finding other work in Nicaragua. More than 60 percent of the people in that country live in poverty, and more than 20 percent of the people of working age are either unemployed or underemployed, able to find only part-time work when they are available to work more often. "We need these jobs," Torres noted, "and we are willing to work very hard. But we also need our rights, that they treat us with dignity and pay us a decent wage that covers at least the basic needs of our families." [37]

Human Rights Agreements Protect Workers' Rights

The types of working conditions Torres endured—long hours, low pay, and no rest—have long been condemned by the international community. In fact, since the 1940s, more than two-thirds of the nations in the world have signed human rights agreements aimed at protecting workers from having to experience such conditions. These agreements include the Universal Declaration, the 1948 Freedom of Association and Protection of the Right to Organize Convention, and the 1966 International Covenant on Economic, Social, and Cultural Rights.

Zenayda Torres (left), a Nicaraguan garment worker, protests low pay and poor working conditions in her industry.

Agreements like these lay out a series of international rights for workers. These include the right of workers to be paid enough money to support themselves and their families, the right to safe working conditions, the right to reasonable limits on the number of hours and days a person works, and the right to form and join trade unions for the protection of one's interests.

Despite widespread recognition of worker's human rights, however, people all over the world continue to endure abusive working conditions. At a conservative estimate, more than five hundred million people—one in six of the working age population—are denied their rights at work.

Human Rights Are Denied to People in Many Industries

People who are denied their rights at work are employed in many different types of jobs. Human rights violations at work are not limited to a certain industry or country. From produce farms to gold mines to garment factories, workers all over the world toil daily in substandard working conditions.

Many farmworkers in Mexico who pick oranges, broccoli, tobacco, cotton, or cut sugarcane, for example, are not paid enough to support themselves and their families. One such worker told a reporter: "No one defends us. [The farm owners] do not pay us what they promised. . . . If the whole family does not work, we all starve."[38] Besides earning such low wages, farmworkers are sometimes exposed to pesticides that can cause cancer, nervous system problems, and, in the case of pregnant farmworkers, birth defects in their children. Mexican farmworkers are therefore regularly denied two internationally recognized human rights: the right to wages adequate to support oneself and one's family, and the right to safe working conditions.

Meanwhile, people doing very different work in a different part of the world are also regularly denied their work-related human rights. Gold, tin, and coal miners in Asia, Africa, and Latin America regularly work in dangerous conditions for low pay. A 1999 report from the International Labour Organization (ILO), an international organization comprising 175 countries, noted that people working at these mines often contract lung disease and other health problems. The ILO report explained:

> The hospital at a large gold mine in Ghana [western Africa] . . . has considerable evidence of widespread silicosis [lung disease] in men, women and children as young as 14 who are engaged in small-scale mining. These are the people who crush gold-bearing ore in their villages using a pestle and mortar . . . no masks are used and the amount of effort required means that the people are breathing deeply, inhaling . . . dust to the maximum on a regular basis. [39]

Adequate pay and limits on working hours are also an issue at mines. In the South American country of Bolivia, for example, the ILO noted that "over 8,000 women work in gold mines north of [the city of] La Paz, where the working conditions . . . are arduous, involving long hours at high altitude, often working in polluted water with no protection for low pay, no social protection [health insurance and unemployment insurance] and no possibility of improvement." [40]

Sweatshops

One group of companies that have become notorious for denying the rights of their workers are companies that manufacture and sell clothing and sneakers. Nike, Adidas, the Gap, and Wal-Mart are just some of the companies that have been the target of protests and scathing reports from human rights activists for their business practices. In particular, these companies have been criticized for having their clothes and sneakers manufactured in factories where the workers sewing and gluing the items together are paid poverty-level wages. Workers are often forced to work long hours with few or no days off. Sometimes, the work is done in rooms with poor ventilation and blocked fire exits, so that the people's health, and even their lives, may be threatened. Factories such as these are typically called sweatshops.

Sweatshops operate in all parts of the world. In El Salvador, for example, a 2001 government report found that "forced overtime, substandard wages, excessive production quotas, abusive and unsafe working conditions, and an animus [hatred] against labor unions prevail in the country's [El Salvador's] 229 . . . factories, which assemble garments for export,"[41] reported the *San Francisco Chronicle*. Likewise, the clothing factories in Bangladesh, a country bordering India in southern Asia, are also well-known for their extremely low pay and abusive working conditions. *New York Times* journalist Barry Bearak noted in April 2001 that the approximately thirty-three hundred "inadequately regulated garment factories [in Bangladesh are] among the worst sweatshops ever to taunt the human conscience."[42] Even in the United States, clothing manufacturers are notorious for violating worker's rights. A recent U.S. Labor Department survey of garment manufacturing shops found that 61 percent of the garment manufacturing shops in Los Angeles and 65 percent of those in New York did not pay their workers minimum or overtime wages. Writing about these statistics in 2001, former U.S. Secretary of Labor Robert Reich remarked:

Bolivian miners haul wagonloads of rocks.

[T]he vast majority of cutting and sewing shops in America's largest cities are sweatshops. . . . When I was secretary of labor I visited garment contractors in several American cities. I saw people crowded together in small spaces with one bathroom and no fire exits, people who hadn't been paid in weeks, sometimes months, and when they were paid it was a mere dollar or two an hour. [43]

Focusing on More Than Clothing Manufacturers

In recent years, clothing and sneaker companies such as Nike, Adidas, the Gap, and Wal-Mart have attracted considerable attention for denying the human rights of the people who manufacture their products. However, the denial of rights at work concerns more than simply the clothing industry. For those working at human rights organizations and at international organizations such as the UN, the rights of all workers in all kinds of jobs are at issue.

Concerned that people may associate worker's rights issues only with clothing and sneaker manufacturers, some human rights groups which originally focused on publicizing the plight of workers in clothing factories have broadened their scope to publicize worker's rights violations in general. The New York–based National Labor Committee (NLC), for example, which has mostly focused on issues of worker's rights within the clothing and sneaker industry, recently released a report criticizing Disney, Hasbro, and other toy manufacturers who make their products in China. The report noted that the factories where these companies' toys are made are essentially sweatshops. The NLC found that people employed at the toy factories were forced to work shifts of fifteen hours or longer for seven days a week with only one day off a month. Workers made as little as twelve cents an hour—below China's legal minimum wage—and worked with toxic chemical glues and paints that often made them dizzy or sick. These conditions are comparable to—if not worse than—the working conditions in many clothing factories worldwide.

Another human rights organization that previously focused on worker's rights within the clothing industry, United Students Against Sweatshops (USAS), has also broadened its emphasis to include workers in all industries. USAS, a group primarily comprised of university students in the United States, now notes on its website that the denial of worker's rights "is not limited to the apparel industry." All struggles for improved worker's rights, USAS now maintains, are "directly or by analogy [symbolically] a struggle against sweatshops,"[44] and therefore of concern to USAS members.

Thus, human rights groups that originally focused on the issue of clothing and sneaker manufacturers today work to inform people that the denial of human rights at work is not only an issue concerning the clothing and sneaker industry. These groups now point out that the toys people buy for their children, the metal used to manufacture household items, even the food on people's tables are also sometimes made, mined, or grown by people toiling under difficult, dangerous, or abusive working conditions.

Reasons People Accept Substandard Working Conditions

To understand why so many workers worldwide accept jobs under such unjust conditions, it is necessary to consider the basic economic conditions of the world today. The World Bank reported in 2000 that, of the world's 6 billion people, "2.8 billion—almost half the world's population—live on less than $2 a day . . . 1.2 billion live on the very margins of life, on less than $1 a day."[45] People living in such poverty do not have enough money to pay for adequate food, shelter, medical care, or the other basic necessities of life.

Moreover, the ILO reports that 80 percent of the world's population has no social protection. Social protection is guaranteed access to the basic necessities of life, usually provided by the government, when citizens cannot earn those necessities themselves. In the United States, for example, social protection includes unemployment insurance; food stamps; welfare; Medicaid insurance, which pays for basic medical care for those who cannot afford it; and social security, which assures an income for the disabled and the elderly.

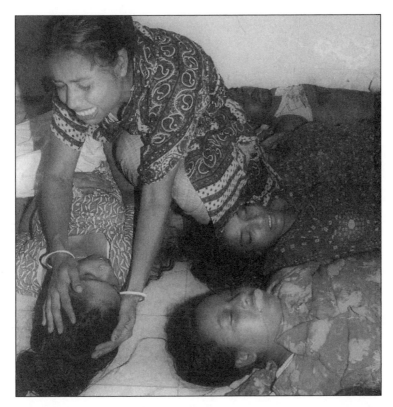

A woman identifies a dead friend, one of dozens killed in a stampede at a textile factory in Bangladesh.

Without social protection, people sometimes face grave dangers, including serious illness and starvation. Of those who have inadequate or no social protection, an estimated 700 million people, more than one in nine worldwide, are chronically hungry. And approximately 500 million of these people, about one in twelve worldwide, have such limited access to food that they are malnourished, meaning they do not have access to enough food to provide a nutritious diet. Malnutrition causes many problems. Malnourished people often suffer from chronic health problems, and they sometimes die from diseases that well-nourished people would be able to withstand.

It is these worldwide conditions that often drive people into dangerous, difficult, or abusive work. People often find that they must choose between abusive conditions of work on the one hand and the possibility of poverty, hunger, homelessness, and related hardships on the other.

The Right to Form Trade Unions

Besides widespread poverty, another factor that contributes to poor working conditions worldwide is the denial, in many countries, of workers' rights to form and join trade unions. Trade unions are organizations that people found with their coworkers and with workers at related companies to promote their interests at work. People traditionally form unions to achieve better pay, safer working conditions, and other improvements at work. When people are allowed to organize unions, they have a better chance of winning work contracts that respect their human rights. The ILO explains: "The right to organize is the key enabling right and the gateway to the exercise of a range of other rights at work."[46] This is because one person insisting on better conditions of work generally has a limited chance of success. But an organized group of workers who can bargain collectively often have enough negotiating power to win improvements at work.

Unions use several techniques to bargain collectively. These techniques include an insistence that all workers have the same contract—so that no group of workers can be singled out for less pay or poorer working conditions. Also, union members may threaten limited or general work stoppages, or strikes, during which time no person in the union works until all workers are given the pay and working conditions desired. The latter technique, however, is typically used only in cases of extreme need; workers themselves suffer if a strike is called since they cannot work during the strike and therefore must do without regular paychecks for the strike's duration.

The right to form and join trade unions has been recognized by most nations. Nevertheless, many workers are still regularly harassed or fired by their employers if they try to join unions. Companies have been known to fire hundreds of workers at a time when workers unionize. Sometimes, workers who try to organize unions are even beaten or jailed. In one instance, at a factory in El Salvador that made clothes for stores like the Gap, Eddie Bauer, and J.C. Penney, a worker reported in an interview that the head of the union was arrested and beaten. "They beat him, tortured him, and threatened him, saying that they would kill his family if he didn't reveal the names of the [union] leaders," the worker explained. Other people were fired for being involved in the union at the factory. The worker remarked: "[T]he company fired more than 350 workers. . . . My two sisters and I were amongst those fired for joining the union."[47]

The Global Compact

Many countries have laws that forbid companies from harassing or firing workers who form or join unions. However, even when national governments genuinely want to enforce such laws, they sometimes find themselves in the difficult position of challenging companies with significant wealth and power. There is increasing concern among human rights organizations, the UN, and human rights scholars that national governments no longer have the power that they used to have to regulate and control the companies that operate within their borders. Some modern corporations—operating in many countries at once—have grown so large that their net worths exceed the budgets of entire nations. This gives the corporations considerable power. They can move their factories from one country to the next if they wish to avoid regulation. Also, they typically wield enough economic clout to influence laws and business regulations within countries. The increasing economic power of these corporations makes it more difficult for national governments to challenge corporations if they violate a country's labor laws. Caroline Thomas, a lecturer in global politics at Southampton University in England, explains: "Under international law, it is the duty of states [national governments] to secure the human rights of their respective citizens . . . but the global economic structure [international structure of business] increasingly renders the state less able to fulfill this duty."[48]

Because of this trend, a new movement to hold companies directly responsible for human rights violations has emerged.

This movement has been led by the 2001 Nobel Peace Prize–winning Secretary General of the UN, Kofi Annan. Annan is championing a new international human rights agreement called the Global Compact, which he and the UN introduced in 1999. The Global Compact is a human rights agreement signed by private companies. The companies that sign the compact pledge to uphold human rights as part of their business practices. The Global Compact emphasizes those human rights most closely related to business practices, including the right of workers to form and join trade unions; the right of people to equal treatment and pay at work, regardless of sex, race, nationality, or religion; and the right of people not to be subjected to forced labor. Besides singling out these work-related human rights, the Compact also states that companies must uphold all other rights described in the 1948 Universal Declaration of Human Rights.

The Global Compact is meant to affect private companies the way the Universal Declaration of Human Rights affected national governments. Once companies have pledged to promote human rights by signing the compact, they will, hopefully, find it harder to make excuses for violating the human rights of their workers. Supporters of the compact hope that these companies will be less likely to argue, as companies sometimes have in the past, that human rights is a political issue best left to governments, and that company executives have no responsibilities to society.

Many businesses have already signed the Global Compact. These include the car manufacturer DaimlerChrysler, the European Deutsche Bank, the oil company BP, and the sporting-goods company Nike. However, since the compact was introduced in 1999, its impact on the daily operations of these companies cannot yet be accurately assessed. Certainly, workers worldwide are still regularly denied their human rights. For example, a 2001 report on Nike workers in Indonesia found their working conditions essentially unchanged from previous years. However, the compact is not designed to have an instant effect on businesses worldwide. It is meant instead to promote a long-term shift in public attitudes toward

Labor activist Dita Sari speaks in front of the Supreme Court of Indonesia. Sari turned down a $50,000 human rights award from Reebok to protest the low wages the company pays to her country's workers.

companies' responsibilities. Supporters hope companies will admit voluntarily that they have a responsibility to promote and protect human rights. This is seen by supporters of the compact as the first step toward the larger and more challenging goal of actually achieving workers' human rights worldwide.

Corporations who have signed the Global Compact and most national governments recognize the rights of people at work as defined by the Universal Declaration of Human Rights. However, hundreds of millions of people worldwide working in all types of industries are still denied their right to decent working conditions. Despite this fact, members of human rights organizations, officials at the UN, and many other people have hopes that sometime in the near future there will be a significant shift in economic conditions, governmental policy, and business practices worldwide, and that many more people will enjoy their economic human rights.

4

Women's Rights Are Human Rights

E QUALITY OF HUMAN rights—regardless of sex or any other distinction—is a central principle recognized in all international human rights agreements. The primary international human rights agreement, the Universal Declaration of Human Rights, expressed this principle with the words: "Everyone is entitled to all the rights and freedoms set forth in this Declaration, without distinction of any kind, such as race, colour, sex, language, religion, political or other opinion, national or social origin, property, birth, or other status."[49]

In recent decades, several international human rights agreements have reiterated this principle of equality in human rights—in particular stressing the equal rights of women and men. One such agreement is the Vienna Declaration and Programme of Action, adopted by 171 UN member countries at the 1993 World Conference on Human Rights. The Vienna Declaration states:

> The human rights of women and of the girl-child are an inalienable, integral and indivisible part of universal human rights. The full and equal participation of women in political, civil, economic, social and cultural life, at the national, regional and international levels, and the eradication of all forms of discrimination on grounds of sex are priority objectives of the international community.[50]

"Facing the Challenge"

Many women's rights activists have expressed concern, however, that international human rights agreements have had only a limited impact on women's lives. Today, women all over the world are regularly denied their human rights. In some countries, women are struggling to win even the most basic human rights, including the right to move freely about their towns and cities, the right to vote and participate in government, the right to equal pay for equal work, and the right to decide whom they will marry. Moreover, women often bear the brunt of widespread, global human rights violations. Seventy percent of the 1.2 billion people who live in severe poverty are women. Women are the majority of the world's refugees and the majority of those who have never been taught how to read and write. Explains human rights activist Sonia Picado Sotela: "International human rights law is facing the challenge of being relevant and credible in improving the circumstances in which the vast majority of the world's women live their lives."[51]

One of the people working to change this situation—to turn the pledges made in international human rights agreements into actions that improve women's lives—is the UN High Commissioner for Human Rights, Mary Robinson. Robinson, formerly the president of Ireland, is a widely respected world leader, often praised by both her UN colleagues and by human rights organizations. As High Commissioner for Human Rights, she oversees all of the UN's human rights efforts, a job that makes her one of the most influential figures working on these rights today.

Writing in 2000 on her efforts to address women's human rights, Robinson noted:

> Practical and creative measures to realize the human rights of women . . . are a priority for my Office and for every part of the United Nations system. . . . I am committed to work in partnership with all United Nations agencies . . . but most specially with women through the world to promote and protect women's rights and to translate these rights into a better quality of life for all.[52]

Female Genital Mutilation

As part of the UN's push to turn the pledges made in international human rights agreements into actions that will improve the lives of women, Robinson has promoted several campaigns focusing on human rights issues that impact

Two Saudi women wear black abaya and veil while walking through a marketplace. Women worldwide suffer the most from human rights violations.

women in particular. One of these campaigns centers in part on a practice that many women's rights activists, particularly in Africa, have decried for years—a practice called female genital mutilation or female circumcision.

Female genital mutilation is a traditional practice in which part or all of a girl's genitalia are cut off. The UN Population Fund reports that every year an estimated 2 million girls and young women undergo female genital mutilation. The practice occurs primarily in certain communities within African countries, including Egypt, Ethiopia, Kenya, and Uganda. Further, some families who have moved from these countries to other parts of the world, such as Western Europe or the United States, also continue the practice. In these cases, parents either find doctors in the new country to perform the mutilation or send their daughters back to their home countries to have the procedure done there. In 2001, the women's health organization FORWARD estimated that as many as fifteen thousand girls in Britain were at risk of undergoing genital mutilation.

Types of Female Genital Mutilation Vary

In African countries, female genital mutilation is often carried out by a woman within the community who also works as a midwife, assisting women during pregnancy and childbirth. The age at which female genital mutilation is done varies. Depending on the community, it may be carried out

Female Genital Mutilation in Africa

ELIMINATE FEMALE GENITAL MUTILATION

A poster protests female genital mutilation.

on girls when they are infants, it may be part of a kind of coming of age ceremony when the girls are around the ages of seven to ten, it may be done on girls only after they reach adolescence, or it may be done on adult women when they marry. Regardless, the procedure typically takes place without anesthesia, and a kitchen knife or razor blade may be used. Many women who recall having the procedure done to them remember it as extremely painful.

The exact type of procedure varies widely from country to country and community to community. In a July 2000 interview, Sudanese-born Dr. Nawal M. Nour, a Harvard-trained doctor and specialist in the subject, described the different types of female genital mutilation:

> [T]ype 1 removes the clitoris, this is common in Ethiopia. Type 2 excises [removes] the clitoris and the inner vaginal lips, which may end up fusing together. Type 3 is removing the clitoris, the inner lips, the outer lips, then sewing everything together, leaving only a very small opening for urination and menses. This is mainly done among Somalis and Sudanese and in parts of West Africa. . . . The women who've undergone Type 3 can have scarring problems and problems with their menses. Some of them

have terrible trouble having sex with their husbands, as you can imagine. . . . This morning, I saw an 18-year-old whose opening was about dime size. I saw a woman the other week who was pregnant and had a pencil-sized opening.[53]

Although all of these procedures also go by the name "female circumcision" instead of "female genital mutilation," none of them is really comparable to the circumcision often carried out on boys. Dr. Nour explains in her interview: "Female circumcision, you see, is nothing like what we know as male circumcision. In the latter, the foreskin is removed from the penis. With female circumcision, we have the equivalent of the penis being removed."[54] Furthermore, while male circumcision typically leads to few if any medical complications, female genital mutilation is associated with many health problems. Women who have undergone the procedure may have difficulty giving birth. They often experience pain during sex. They also often have scarring and sometimes infections arise because of the procedure. And girls sometimes experience severe bleeding immediately after undergoing the mutilation. Some girls have died from such bleeding.

Reasons Female Genital Mutilation Continues

Supporters of female genital mutilation give many reasons for the continuation of the practice. Parents often have female genital mutilation carried out on their daughters because girls are not considered good prospects for marriage until they undergo the procedure. In addition, female genital mutilation is often said to keep a girl chaste, suppressing her sexual desire and ensuring that she remain a virgin until marriage. Also, members of some communities argue that female genital mutilation is part of the Islamic religion. However, the practice is not contemplated by the vast majority of Muslims worldwide. Rather, it is mostly confined to certain regions of Africa, and it is carried out by Christian communities in these regions as well.

Aminata Diop, a woman who fled home to avoid undergoing the procedure, explains why her family wanted her to have it done:

[M]y mother thought it was a religious necessity. . . . She thought the Koran [the Muslim holy book] demanded that parents have their daughters excised so they will be clean and be

A nineteen-year-old girl who escaped genital mutilation in her African homeland is overcome with emotion.

good Muslims . . . my mother said a woman has to go through three ordeals in life: we must go through excision [female genital mutilation], marriage, and giving birth. Excision is a woman's destiny. [55]

Besides confronting this attitude among her family, Diop also encountered a similar sentiment from her fiancé. "I explained to my fiancé that I was frightened; I told him how painful it would be . . . he said he could not accept it [that Diop had not undergone the procedure]. . . . He said he could not be proud of a woman who would be dirty . . . he would be ashamed. He let me down. . . . He reacted just like my parents." [56] Despite these pressures, Diop decided not to undergo the procedure and was able to avoid it by fleeing to France.

Campaigns to End Female Genital Mutilation

Because female genital mutilation has such potentially extreme consequences for the health of girls and women, and because as many as 2 million girls and young women undergo the procedure every year, efforts to stop female genital mutilation have been taken up worldwide and are considered a priority by many women's rights activists, human rights organizations, and the UN. Spreading information about the health problems associated with mutilation, persuading religious leaders to state publicly that female genital mutilation is not a religious act, and supporting teenagers and young women who refuse to undergo the procedure are all central aspects of the struggle to end female genital mutilation. Henriette Kouyate, a Senegalese doctor who has been working against female genital mutilation since 1955, explains:

> We have seminars for people in positions of responsibility: midwives, doctors, cultural advisers. We ask them to spread information and to make the population aware [of the health risks of mutilation]. . . . We also had a seminar for people performing circumcisions. . . . Our task was to explain to them the harmful side . . . to explain that they are not obliged to do this and that it is not a religious obligation, and to show that it is not possible to perform a circumcision without causing harm. [57]

In Kenya, one campaign to end the practice among that country's Marakwet ethnic group has had good success. There, the people kept the initiation rites that accompany female genital mutilation but stopped performing the actual procedure, making the ceremony symbolic only. Statistics gathered in 1999 suggest that fewer than two hundred Marakwet girls that year underwent actual cutting of the genitals, whereas more than ten thousand girls did so in the previous four years.

Other countries have outlawed the practice altogether. Female genital mutilation has recently been banned in Ghana, Kenya, and Senegal, among other countries, and in Egypt it can be performed legally only with a prescription from a doctor. There is some concern among those working against female genital mutilation, however, that making the procedure illegal could drive it underground and actually make it more difficult to eliminate in the long term. A UN expert working on the issue explains:

> Punishments and [jail] sentences . . . could sometimes be counter-productive and encourage communities to close ranks and cling to [traditional] practices. Such practices should not be condemned in the courts except as a last resort when education, information and the proposal of alternative rites that do not injure women and girls have not been successful.[58]

Even so, as a result of these efforts, female genital mutilation does appear to be on the decline. However, that decline is far too slow for human rights activists, who are concerned with each of the millions of girls who undergo the irreversible procedure every year.

Human Trafficking

Female genital mutilation is considered a human rights issue because the practice violates internationally recognized rights to personal security, to integrity of a person's body, and to basic health. A similar push has taken place in recent years with regard to another issue that impacts the health and personal security of millions of women and girls every year: the trafficking of women and girls across borders to work in sweatshops, as domestic servants, and as prostitutes. Trafficking humans involves smuggling people either from one

Prostitutes await customers near the German–Czechoslovakian border. Worldwide, many thousands of women and children are forced into prostitution each year.

part of a country to another or across national borders for the purpose of using them as forced or exploited labor.

Today, hundreds of thousands of women and children are trafficked every year. Many of those trafficked are teenage girls. The U.S. State Department estimated in 2001 that 700,000 women and children are trafficked across international borders annually, while the European Union estimates that 120,000 women and children are trafficked into Western Europe each year; many of those come from Eastern Europe and the former Soviet Union. Furthermore, the U.S. State Department estimates that 45,000 to 50,000 women and children are trafficked into the United States each year. Approximately half of the women and children trafficked into the United States "are forced into sweatshop labor and domestic servitude," the State Department reports. "The rest are [mostly] forced into prostitution and the sex industry." [59]

"The Opportunity to Work"

Trafficking usually starts in a country, called a sending country, where the levels of poverty are high and jobs are difficult to come by. Sending countries include Russia, Thailand, and Mexico. Many young women in these countries are looking for work to help them support themselves and their families. Traffickers—people working in small criminal networks who arrange the move and profit from the practice— offer these women the opportunity to work abroad, typically misrepresenting the terms of the work or lying outright about what the work will entail. Some women, for example, may be told that the work involves prostitution, garment-factory work, or domestic work, but are misled about the realities of the treatment they will encounter when they arrive in the destination country. Others are simply told outright lies; they may be told, for example, that they will work as models, hostesses in bars, or secretaries, when in reality they are being sent to work as prostitutes.

Once the women have agreed to move, the traffickers then make all the travel arrangements. They arrange transportation and obtain visas and passports. Sometimes they arrange illegal ways to get past immigration officials, such as crossing a border hidden on a truck or ship.

When the women arrive in the new country, they find themselves in debt to the traffickers for arranging their transportation and entry into the country. The traffickers then force them into jobs to pay off this debt. Sometimes, traffickers hold the women's passports so that they have no form of identification in the country, other times they threaten the women with physical violence if the women try to leave their jobs. Women are also often told that if they go to the police or end up arrested for prostitution, they will be sent back to their home countries.

A twenty-seven-year-old woman who was trafficked from the east Asian country of Thailand into prostitution in Japan recounts her experience:

> A friend I knew from the market . . . told me about the opportunity to work in factories in Japan . . . my son was three years old and I had to raise him by myself and was finding it difficult to make enough money. . . . I was told by the recruiters in Thailand that I would work in a factory and would get fifty percent of my salary until my debt was paid off . . . [I] did not realize that we [she and other women being trafficked with her] were being sold into prostitution. [60]

This woman arrived in Japan in debt to her traffickers for the equivalent of more than twenty thousand dollars. She explains:

> I worked [in Japan] for eight months [as a prostitute] to pay back my debt. . . . I had calculated that I must have paid it back long ago, but the mama [manager] kept lying to me and said she didn't have the same records as I did. During these eight months, I had to take every client that wanted me and had to work every day, even during my menstruation. . . . The [manager] threatened me, saying that if I made any trouble she'd sell me again and double my debt. During the first three months I was never allowed out of the apartment except with the [manager] or a client. [61]

Human Trafficking Involves More Than Prostitution

Although trafficking for the sex industry is the most widely publicized form of human trafficking, women and girls are also trafficked to keep a supply of maids, nannies, and sweatshop laborers coming into a country. Women are often

brought from the Southeast Asian countries of Indonesia and the Philippines to work as maids and nannies in Saudi Arabia, for example, without fully understanding the conditions of such work. These women may be made to work extremely long hours at low pay; they sometimes even endure physical abuse from their employers. The human rights group Amnesty International noted in September 2000 that women working as domestic servants in Saudi Arabia are "often locked in the homes of their employers."[62] As foreigners working in the isolated environment of a family's home, they are particularly vulnerable to abusive treatment. One woman told Amnesty: "I was regularly spat at by all members of the family, and beaten, usually by the father. . . . The beatings began when I had been in the house for three months. I asked for my salary as at that point I had received nothing. . . . From that point, I was beaten every day."[63]

In the United States, meanwhile, women are sometimes trafficked into the country and then forced into exploitative jobs in garment factories. Like other trafficked women, these women typically start work already deeply indebted to their employers. They may have their passports held by their employers to keep them from leaving their jobs. And some may also be told that they will be sent back to their home countries if they go to the police or otherwise come to the attention of authorities by protesting against their working conditions.

"The Rights of Women Are Central to Our Vision"

The problems of human trafficking and female genital mutilation are two issues that involve the violation of women's human rights. Today, these and other women's rights issues have become central human rights issues. UN High Commissioner for Human Rights Mary Robinson explains:

> Women's equal dignity and human rights as full human beings are enshrined in the basic instruments of today's international community. From the Charter of the United Nations' endorsement of the equal rights of men and women, to the Universal Declaration of Human Rights and the subsequent international treaties and declarations, the rights of women are central to our vision of a democratic society. . . . There can be no peace, security or sustainable economic development in societies which deny human rights, including the rights of women. I believe this is gradually being understood by governments. [64]

5

Strategies to Promote Human Rights

GOVERNMENTS TODAY REGULARLY violate their pledges to uphold human rights within their countries and to promote human rights for all people worldwide. Thus, over the past fifty years, those concerned with human rights have tried many strategies to push governments to uphold these pledges. Some people use protests and street demonstrations to call attention to human rights issues. Others work as politicians or public servants within governments to change laws or public policies. And many people work for nonprofit organizations that focus on human rights issues at the local, national, or international level.

Human Rights Activists

At the heart of all efforts to promote human rights are the people who dedicate their own time and energy to enact change. People who do so are generally called human rights activists. Human rights activists work on many issues, from government brutality to poor working conditions; what unites these activists is that they look to the vision described in international human rights agreements for inspiration.

Each activist furthers human rights in her or his own way: through day-to-day work, dedicating private time, making sacrifices in life, and in some cases risking personal harm. "A few such people [activists] become known to the general public; the vast majority of them toil without international recognition," explains UN High Commissioner for Human

Rights Mary Robinson. "But what they all have in common is a willingness to work for human rights values, even at the expense of their own comfort."[65]

Robinson and many others who work on human rights issues maintain that little progress could be made without the effort of human rights activists. If no person were to put his or her time and energy into working for progress on human rights, they argue, how would such progress occur? Egyptian human rights activist Hafez Al Sayed Seada expressed this view in a 2000 interview: "If we don't start now, the next generation will inherit our failure to bring about change. . . . I know that the future will see an Egypt becoming more democratic, with respect for human rights. But this is the future only if people demand their rights and they struggle."[66]

Mexicans remember slain human rights lawyer Digna Ochoa. Many activists have lost their lives in the struggle for human rights.

Grassroots Human Rights Groups

Human rights activists often establish or join organizations to aid and support one another, together accomplishing what one person working alone could not. All over the world, countless small human rights organizations, often staffed by volunteers, work daily to protect people's human rights and to publicize human rights issues. Cambodian human rights activist Kek Galabru recalls starting one such group, the Cambodian League for the Promotion and Defense of Human Rights, in the early 1990s: "We didn't have any money, so we opened a small office at my parents' home."[67]

These groups—often called "grassroots" human rights groups—operate in almost every country. They include the Ixcán Association for Human Rights in the Ixcán region of Guatemala, the group Haitian Women in Solidarity that works in the Caribbean nation of Haiti, the San Francisco–based Bay Area Police Watch in the United States, and the human rights group B'Tselem in Israel.

Grassroots human rights organizations are considered central to efforts to promote human rights because they work at the local level. Pakistani human rights activist Hina Jilani explains why she believes grassroots work is so important: "A human rights defender in the field is a foot soldier. We are the ones who will make a difference."[68] UN human rights worker Gertrude Mongella echoes Jilani's sentiment. "We can't get anything accomplished without working at the grass roots."[69]

International Human Rights Groups

Larger, international human rights organizations are also extremely important. Such groups can publicize human rights issues to the broader international community and mobilize support worldwide in a way that grassroots organizations cannot.

One of the most prominent large human rights organizations is the London-based group Amnesty International. Amnesty was founded in 1961 by British lawyer Peter Benenson. Initially, Benenson conceived of the idea of mass letter-writing campaigns, conducted by ordinary people, on behalf of prisoners of conscience. Benenson thought of the

Amnesty International demonstrators protest for a free Tibet.

concept after hearing about two Portuguese students who had been imprisoned for toasting to freedom under the dictator António de Oliveira Salazar.

Today, Amnesty has offices in more than fifty countries and territories, and close to a million supporters worldwide. Amnesty's activities include public demonstrations, investigations into instances of human rights abuses, giving testimony before the UN Human Rights Commissions, releasing country-by-country annual reports describing human rights violations, and fund-raising for human rights causes. Amnesty has also continued its letter-writing campaigns on behalf of prisoners of conscience. These campaigns have been instrumental in the release of prisoners all over the world. In an interview with journalist Jonathan Power, Nigerian president Olusegun Obasanjo, who was once a prisoner of conscience himself, described the effects of Amnesty's letter-writing campaigns in his country:

> It's like constant drips of water on a stone. It seems to make little difference, but over time it does. I think it did three important things: it gave a lot of prisoners who didn't have a well-known name a lot of hope; it wore at the nerves of the jailers and senior policemen, so when change came they were more or less ready for it; and it helped keep awake Western governments on the job of pushing Nigeria [to free prisoners of conscience].[70]

Amnesty International is only one of many large, international organizations working to improve human rights. Another prominent human rights group is Human Rights Watch, based in Washington, D.C. Human Rights Watch, like Amnesty, focuses on documenting and publicizing human rights abuses worldwide and calling for action in these cases. A third prominent human rights group is Oxfam International. Oxfam has offices in twelve countries and focuses primarily on poverty and economic rights. Oxfam raises money for humanitarian efforts worldwide and, its website explains, works for "[c]hange in a world where hundreds of millions do not have the right to sufficient food, clean water, shelter or security, or the right to speak out against this injustice."[71]

Economic Divestment

The changes sought by human rights activists and organizations are often huge in scale. Activists may seek an end to the human rights abuses of an entire government. They may challenge the practices of multinational companies whose profits exceed the budgets of whole nations. Or they may seek to transform cultural practices that have stood for centuries, such as racial oppression or the denial of equal rights to women. Because these changes are often so sweeping, the methods activists and organizations propose to further their human rights struggles are often equally large in scale.

One method that has been used to promote human rights, for instance, has been to single out a certain country for international economic divestment, or sanctions. International economic divestment against a country occurs when business and trade with that country are restricted or stopped by other countries or by international organizations such as the UN. The hope behind such a tactic is that a government that is abusing human rights will ultimately stop those abuses in order to end the economic restrictions.

The most famous success of economic divestment occurred in the 1980s when many countries, and even individual investors, decided to restrict their business with South Africa. The government of South Africa at the time was based on a policy of racial discrimination called apartheid, literally "apart-ness." Under the apartheid government, only whites were allowed to vote. Many jobs were designated white only. Black Africans were forced onto small tracts of land called homelands. When they left these homelands to work, shop, or travel in the rest of the country, they were forced to carry passes, similar to passports, as if they were foreigners in their own land.

Outrage at this racist apartheid government led activists in Western Europe, the United States, and other parts of the world to call for economic divestment from that country. As a result, many nations passed laws restricting trade with South Africa. The United States, for example, passed the Comprehensive Anti-Apartheid Act of 1986, prohibiting "any U.S. national [citizen] from making any new investment in South Africa" except for investments in "firms owned by black South Africans," and banning "the importation [into the United States] of any article grown, produced, or manufactured by . . . an organization owned or controlled by the South African Government."[72]

Ultimately, the economic pressure caused by these sanctions helped bring an end to South Africa's apartheid government. In 1994, it was replaced by a democratic government guaranteeing equal rights for all citizens without regard to race. Economic sanctions against South Africa therefore proved to be successful.

The Courts

Another method used to pressure governments into ending human rights abuses is the use of national and international courts to try human rights violators. Many international human rights agreements are legal documents that can be used as the basis for claims in court.

One example of such an agreement is the Convention Against Torture and Other Cruel, Inhuman or Degrading Treatment or Punishment. The Convention Against Torture makes torture an international crime. In particular, the convention makes torture an extraditable offense, which means one country can request that another country arrest an alleged torturer—assuming that there is sufficient evidence—and send the person to the first country for trial.

In 1999, two countries used the Convention Against Torture to pursue legal action against a notorious torturer, General Augusto Pinochet, who regularly used torture during his rule in Chile from 1973 to 1989. First, a Spanish judge issued

General Pinochet (pictured) is accused of human rights violations while ruling Chile.

an extradition request for the arrest of Pinochet. The judge's request was done on behalf of Spanish citizens who had been tortured while living in Chile under Pinochet's rule. Then, the government of Britain, acting on Spain's extradition request, arrested General Pinochet when he traveled to Britain on a personal trip. Britain and Spain surprised political observers when they acted against General Pinochet, because former dictators—no matter how brutal their regimes—have traditionally been allowed to live freely after stepping down from their rule.

General Pinochet challenged the legality of his arrest, and, because the British government had relied on the relatively new Convention Against Torture to arrest him, Pinochet's challenge was heard by the top justices in that country, the Law Lords of the Parliament's House of Lords. For a time, while the Law Lords heard the case, human rights activists everywhere—and many people in Chile—waited nervously, concerned that the Lords might overrule the arrest and order the British government to free Pinochet. The Law Lords ultimately affirmed the arrest, however, ruling that the Convention Against Torture did allow Britain to arrest Pinochet and extradite him to Spain. Human rights activists worldwide cheered the decision.

Spain never would see Pinochet, however, because, just before the extradition was to take place, the British government declared that Pinochet was too sick to stand trial and therefore should be sent home to Chile. Many human rights activists saw this as backpedaling on the part of the British government, since despite the Law Lords' decision affirming the legality of the arrest, the government ultimately decided on its own not to go through with the extradition. Nevertheless, the arrest of Pinochet in Britain and the ruling of the Law Lords upholding the arrest was still seen as a tremendous victory for human rights. "Whatever the outcome of the Pinochet case, it has altered world law," writes law professor and human rights activist Robert Drinan. "It has made clear that those who torture or engage in other offences forbidden by world law can be tried in any nation to which they travel."[73] Today, the precedent has been set for further arrests and proceedings against those who commit torture, no matter where in the world they are.

Debt Relief

Economic sanctions and trials based on international law are two methods that have been used to promote international human rights. However, there are some human rights abuses that call for very different strategies. Specifically, abuses related to the right of all people to food, clothing, shelter, and medical care—sometimes thought of as the right not to live in poverty—do not seem well suited to solutions such as trials or economic sanctions.

Today, hundreds of millions of people worldwide are severely impoverished. Improving this situation is considered one of the world's greatest human rights challenges. One strategy that has recently been proposed to help address this issue is called debt relief.

Currently, many countries borrow money from international and foreign lenders to supplement their annual budgets. These lenders include commercial banks, foreign governments, and international institutions such as the World Bank and the International Monetary Fund (IMF). Wealthier countries are able to pay back this debt over time without significantly impacting their citizens' access to food, clothing, shelter, and health care. However, many developing countries today owe debts that have started to overwhelm their national budgets. The central African country of Zambia, for example, spent approximately a quarter of its national budget on foreign debt in 2001. And that same year the countries of Gambia, Guyana, Nicaragua, São Tomé and Principe, and Senegal spent between 15 and 20 percent of their government revenues on debt.

Because these and other countries have to pay so much money to foreign lenders each year, they do not have enough money left to uphold the economic and social rights of their citizens. Oxfam reported in 2001, for example, that Zambia spends more on debt than on health care for its citizens. "This in a country where one out of five children will not live to see their 5th birthday, and where the impact of the HIV/AIDS crisis has reduced life expectancy to 40 years,"[74] the Oxfam report explained. Oxfam maintains that "these massive debts [should] be forgiven so that poor countries can spend their money on domestic needs—education, health care, and social services—rather than servicing [paying off] their debts."[75] Thus, many human rights organizations have argued for some form of debt relief.

Heeding this call, the international community has accepted limited debt relief as a way to reduce poverty. In 1996, the World Bank and the IMF introduced a program, called the Debt Initiative for Heavily Indebted Poor Countries (HIPC), to forgive some of the debt of impoverished countries. The countries that are selected to participate in this program will have to pay back only some of the money that they owe to the World Bank, the IMF, and other lenders. Twenty-four countries are now receiving debt relief through HIPC, including the Latin American countries of Bolivia, Honduras, and Nicaragua, and the African countries of Ethiopia, Madagascar, Mozambique, and Rwanda. As a result, the World Bank expects spending on social programs such as health care and education to increase in these countries. A World Bank report released in March 2002 estimated that "[i]ncreases in education and health spending are expected to absorb about two-thirds of the total relief, with about 40 percent directed towards education and 25 percent to health care."[76]

Linking Foreign Policy to Human Rights

On March 10, 1999, in Guatemala City, Guatemala, U.S. president Bill Clinton made an admission that was welcomed by human rights activists and organizations. "For the United States, it is important that I state clearly that support for military forces or intelligence units which engaged in violent and widespread repression . . . was wrong," he said during a speech, "and the United States must not repeat that mistake."[77] The support that Clinton was referring to was military support, military training, and diplomatic support

President Bill Clinton stands alongside President Alvaro Arzu of Guatemala. In a speech during his visit, Clinton admitted that U.S. support for the violent Guatemalan government of the 1980s was wrong.

President Bill Clinton stands alongside President Alvaro Arzu of Guatemala. In a speech during his visit, Clinton admitted that U.S. support for the violent Guatemalan government of the 1980s was wrong.

the United States had given to the government of Guatemala in the early 1980s. During that time, the Guatamalan government was torturing, secretly abducting, and executing people in that country.

Clinton's admission that U.S. support for this regime was wrong held tremendous importance not only to the survivors of that regime and the families of those who had been abducted or killed, but also to human rights activists and organizations worldwide. Human rights advocates regularly express frustration when one or several countries support a government that is engaged in severe human rights abuses. "No American wants his or her hard-earned money [paid in taxes] used to harm innocent people," explains executive director of Amnesty International USA William Schulz. "Surely we have better things to do with our money."[78]

Difficult in Practice

Many governments that violate human rights receive military, economic, and diplomatic support from other countries. The Taliban government of Afghanistan received support from its neighbor Pakistan, for example. And North Korea, another government known for its human rights violations, has regularly been supplied with arms by China. Human rights advocates believe that ending such support would go a long way toward ending human rights violations. However, governments generally place self-interest, self-preservation, or support for a political, economic, or religious ideal over the protection of human rights. During the Cold War, for example, the U.S.S.R. supported governments—even repressive ones—if the countries remained allied with the U.S.S.R. and rejected ties to Western Europe and the United States. Likewise, Western Europe and the United States supported governments—even repressive ones—as long as they were anticommunist. Although such a political strategy does not necessarily rule out the possibility of promoting human rights in other countries, it allows for the support of human rights only if such actions do not seriously interfere with other political concerns. This is because the political, economic, or security concerns of a nation are considered by the governments involved to be more important than international human rights.

Embrace of such a foreign policy strategy, however, often contradicts the pledges that governments have made to uphold human rights. Even though in certain instances of national emergency, countries may have no option but to support a government that violates human rights, human rights advocates generally argue that these instances account for only a small fraction of the times countries support such human rights abusers. More typically, advocates contend, support of governments that violate human rights is driven by economic, ideological, or geopolitical concerns.

Advocates argue that such foreign policy strategies should be reconsidered. Support for human rights should be pursued whenever possible, they contend, not only as a moral imperative but also as a practical way to promote

Iraq's president Saddam Hussein had U.S. support throughout the 1980s, despite public knowledge of human rights abuses.

national and international security. In fact, advocates say, support for governments that violate human rights often creates security problems in the long term.

As one of many examples, human rights advocates point to the economic and political support that the United States gave to Iraqi president Saddam Hussein in the 1980s, both during and after Iraq's eight-year war with its neighbor Iran. At the time, the Iraqi government regularly committed severe human rights abuses, and the U.S. State Department openly acknowledged the fact. However, U.S. foreign policy experts believed economic and political support for Iraq was necessary for several reasons, including the perceived need to balance Iran's power in the region. Support for Iraq also had economic benefits for the United States. The U.S. government was therefore willing to support Iraq despite its human rights abuses; those abuses included the Iraqi government's use of chemical weapons against its own citizens in 1988.

Meanwhile, because of Iraqi human rights abuses, human rights advocates at the time called for an end to support for Iraq, or at the minimum a U.S. foreign policy that tied American support to improvements in human rights within Iraq. However, the U.S. government ignored these calls. Although there were disputes within the government about the policy at the time, the U.S. government went ahead and doubled funding for its agricultural aid to Iraq in 1989. In October 1989, U.S. Assistant Secretary of State John Kelly noted: "Iraq is an important state [country] with great potential. We want to deepen and broaden our relationship [with Iraq]."[79]

Many U.S. foreign policy experts therefore reasoned in the 1980s that there were good political and economic reasons to support President Hussein's government in Iraq. However, this support also helped to strengthen Hussein's government. In 1990, U.S. policy backfired when the United States was faced with a military crisis involving Hussein's government. Iraq invaded Kuwait, a small country on Iraq's southern border, and shortly afterward the United States made the decision to go to war with Iraq. Today, the Iraqi government is considered by U.S. foreign policy analysts to be one of the most dangerous security threats in the world. Human rights advocates point to this example and argue that if human rights concerns had been considered more important from the outset, this potential threat to U.S. and world security might have been avoided.

Supporting Those Who Support Human Rights

Placing human rights in the center of foreign policy, as proposed by human rights advocates, not only means ending military, economic, and diplomatic support for governments that violate human rights, it also means increasing support for governments that respect human rights. Human rights proponents maintain that such a strategy would be a practical foreign policy, and that it would promote the national and international security of all peaceful nations.

Those in favor of international human rights have always held that respect for human rights is the key to peace. Repression, brutality, poverty, and discrimination within countries, they argue, inevitably makes those countries unstable and leads to war and violence. In fact, the international human rights movement arose amid the violence and destruction of World War II with the express purpose of promoting world peace. Thus, for those in favor of human rights, a foreign policy that promotes human rights as its central goal is, by definition, a foreign policy that promotes national and international security. Peace and human rights, they maintain, go hand in hand.

Economic embargoes are one tactic for fighting human rights abuses, but they can also contribute to poverty, malnutrition, and illness among people who live in the country facing embargo.

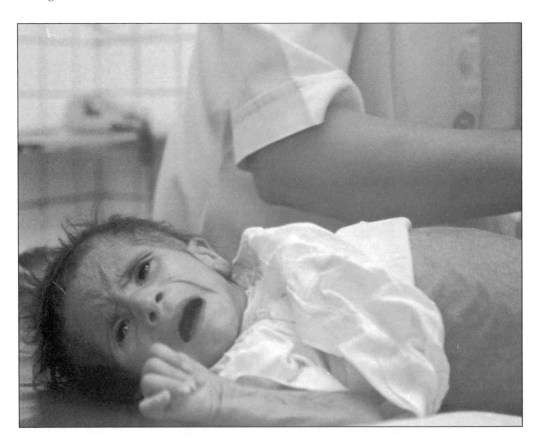

"Working and Struggling Is How You Become Happy"

Considering the size and scope of human rights issues, few if any of the people working to further human rights worldwide expect the solutions to be simple. To the contrary, many human rights activists assume that human rights will continue to be an issue well beyond their own lifetimes.

Nevertheless, people all over the world continue to struggle in ways large and small to further international respect for human rights. In a 2000 interview with author Kerry Kennedy Cuomo, Turkish human rights activist Senal Sarihan described her reasons for continuing the human rights struggle: "Courage is a way of life. Working and struggling is how you become happy. When you look back on your life, you should have changed the world somehow."[80]

Appendix:

Text of the Universal Declaration of Human Rights

Adopted and proclaimed by General Assembly resolution 217 A (III) of 10 December 1948

PREAMBLE

Whereas recognition of the inherent dignity and of the equal and inalienable rights of all members of the human family is the foundation of freedom, justice and peace in the world,

Whereas disregard and contempt for human rights have resulted in barbarous acts which have outraged the conscience of mankind, and the advent of a world in which human beings shall enjoy freedom of speech and belief and freedom from fear and want has been proclaimed as the highest aspiration of the common people,

Whereas it is essential, if man is not to be compelled to have recourse, as a last resort, to rebellion against tyranny and oppression, that human rights should be protected by the rule of law,

Whereas it is essential to promote the development of friendly relations between nations,

Whereas the peoples of the United Nations have in the Charter reaffirmed their faith in fundamental human rights, in the dignity and worth of the human person and in the equal rights of men and women and have determined to promote social progress and better standards of life in larger freedom,

Whereas Member States have pledged themselves to achieve, in co-operation with the United Nations, the promotion of universal respect for and observance of human rights and fundamental freedoms,

Whereas a common understanding of these rights and freedoms is of the greatest importance for the full realization of this pledge,

Now, Therefore THE GENERAL ASSEMBLY proclaims THIS UNIVERSAL DECLARATION OF HUMAN RIGHTS as a common standard of achievement for all peoples and all nations, to the end that every individual and every organ of society, keeping this Declaration constantly in mind, shall strive by teaching and education to promote respect for these rights and freedoms and by progressive measures, national and international, to secure their universal and effective recognition and observance, both among the peoples of Member States themselves and among the peoples of territories under their jurisdiction.

Article 1.
All human beings are born free and equal in dignity and rights. They are endowed with reason and conscience and should act towards one another in a spirit of brotherhood.

Article 2.
Everyone is entitled to all the rights and freedoms set forth in this Declaration, without distinction of any kind, such as race, colour, sex, language, religion, political or other opinion, national or social origin, property, birth or other status. Furthermore, no distinction shall be made on the basis of the political, jurisdictional or international status of the country or territory to which a person belongs, whether it be independent, trust, non-self-governing or under any other limitation of sovereignty.

Article 3.
Everyone has the right to life, liberty and security of person.

Article 4.
No one shall be held in slavery or servitude; slavery and the slave trade shall be prohibited in all their forms.

Article 5.
No one shall be subjected to torture or to cruel, inhuman or degrading treatment or punishment.

Article 6.

Everyone has the right to recognition everywhere as a person before the law.

Article 7.

All are equal before the law and are entitled without any discrimination to equal protection of the law. All are entitled to equal protection against any discrimination in violation of this Declaration and against any incitement to such discrimination.

Article 8.

Everyone has the right to an effective remedy by the competent national tribunals for acts violating the fundamental rights granted him by the constitution or by law.

Article 9.

No one shall be subjected to arbitrary arrest, detention or exile.

Article 10.

Everyone is entitled in full equality to a fair and public hearing by an independent and impartial tribunal, in the determination of his rights and obligations and of any criminal charge against him.

Article 11.

(1) Everyone charged with a penal offence has the right to be presumed innocent until proved guilty according to law in a public trial at which he has had all the guarantees necessary for his defense.

(2) No one shall be held guilty of any penal offence on account of any act or omission which did not constitute a penal offence, under national or international law, at the time when it was committed. Nor shall a heavier penalty be imposed than the one that was applicable at the time the penal offence was committed.

Article 12.

No one shall be subjected to arbitrary interference with his privacy, family, home or correspondence, nor to attacks upon his honour and reputation. Everyone has the right to the protection of the law against such interference or attacks.

Article 13.

(1) Everyone has the right to freedom of movement and residence within the borders of each state.

(2) Everyone has the right to leave any country, including his own, and to return to his country.

Article 14.

(1) Everyone has the right to seek and to enjoy in other countries asylum from persecution.

(2) This right may not be invoked in the case of prosecutions genuinely arising from non-political crimes or from acts contrary to the purposes and principles of the United Nations.

Article 15.

(1) Everyone has the right to a nationality.

(2) No one shall be arbitrarily deprived of his nationality nor denied the right to change his nationality.

Article 16.

(1) Men and women of full age, without any limitation due to race, nationality or religion, have the right to marry and to found a family. They are entitled to equal rights as to marriage, during marriage and at its dissolution.

(2) Marriage shall be entered into only with the free and full consent of the intending spouses.

(3) The family is the natural and fundamental group unit of society and is entitled to protection by society and the State.

Article 17.

(1) Everyone has the right to own property alone as well as in association with others.

(2) No one shall be arbitrarily deprived of his property.

Article 18.

Everyone has the right to freedom of thought, conscience and religion; this right includes freedom to change his religion or belief, and freedom, either alone or in community with others and in public or private, to manifest his religion or belief in teaching, practice, worship and observance.

Article 19.

Everyone has the right to freedom of opinion and expression; this right includes freedom to hold opinions without interference and to seek, receive and impart information and ideas through any media and regardless of frontiers.

Article 20.

(1) Everyone has the right to freedom of peaceful assembly and association.

(2) No one may be compelled to belong to an association.

Article 21.

(1) Everyone has the right to take part in the government of his country, directly or through freely chosen representatives.

(2) Everyone has the right of equal access to public service in his country.

(3) The will of the people shall be the basis of the authority of government; this will shall be expressed in periodic and genuine elections which shall be by universal and equal suffrage and shall be held by secret vote or by equivalent free voting procedures.

Article 22.

Everyone, as a member of society, has the right to social security and is entitled to realization, through national effort and international co-operation and in accordance with the organization and resources of each State, of the economic, social and cultural rights indispensable for his dignity and the free development of his personality.

Article 23.

(1) Everyone has the right to work, to free choice of employment, to just and favourable conditions of work and to protection against unemployment.

(2) Everyone, without any discrimination, has the right to equal pay for equal work.

(3) Everyone who works has the right to just and favourable remuneration ensuring for himself and his family an existence worthy of human dignity, and supplemented, if necessary, by other means of social protection.

(4) Everyone has the right to form and to join trade unions for the protection of his interests.

Article 24.

Everyone has the right to rest and leisure, including reasonable limitation of working hours and periodic holidays with pay.

Article 25.

(1) Everyone has the right to a standard of living adequate for the health and well-being of himself and of his family, including food, clothing, housing and medical care and necessary social services, and the right to security in the event of unemployment, sickness, disability, widowhood, old age or other lack of livelihood in circumstances beyond his control.

(2) Motherhood and childhood are entitled to special care and assistance. All children, whether born in or out of wedlock, shall enjoy the same social protection.

Article 26.

(1) Everyone has the right to education. Education shall be free, at least in the elementary and fundamental stages. Elementary education shall be compulsory. Technical and professional education shall be made generally available and higher education shall be equally accessible to all on the basis of merit.

(2) Education shall be directed to the full development of the human personality and to the strengthening of respect for human rights and fundamental freedoms. It shall promote understanding, tolerance and friendship among all nations, racial or religious groups, and shall further the activities of the United Nations for the maintenance of peace.

(3) Parents have a prior right to choose the kind of education that shall be given to their children.

Article 27.

(1) Everyone has the right freely to participate in the cultural life of the community, to enjoy the arts and to share in scientific advancement and its benefits.

(2) Everyone has the right to the protection of the moral and material interests resulting from any scientific, literary or artistic production of which he is the author.

Article 28.

Everyone is entitled to a social and international order in which the rights and freedoms set forth in this Declaration can be fully realized.

Article 29.

(1) Everyone has duties to the community in which alone the free and full development of his personality is possible.

(2) In the exercise of his rights and freedoms, everyone shall be subject only to such limitations as are determined by law solely for the purpose of securing due recognition and respect for the rights and freedoms of others and of meeting the just requirements of morality, public order and the general welfare in a democratic society.

(3) These rights and freedoms may in no case be exercised contrary to the purposes and principles of the United Nations.

Article 30.

Nothing in this Declaration may be interpreted as implying for any State, group or person any right to engage in any activity or to perform any act aimed at the destruction of any of the rights and freedoms set forth herein.

Notes

Introduction

1. Richard A. Falk, *Human Rights Horizons.* New York: Routledge, 2000, p. 2.

Chapter 1: The Universal Declaration of Human Rights

2. United Nations, "Universal Declaration of Human Rights," December 10, 1948, art. 1. www.un.org.

3. Quoted in Mary Ann Glendon, *A World Made New: Eleanor Roosevelt and the Universal Declaration of Human Rights.* New York: Random House, 2001, p. 208.

4. Johannes Morsink, *The Universal Declaration of Human Rights: Origins, Drafting and Intent.* Philadelphia: University of Pennsylvania Press, 1999, p. x.

5. Quoted in Lois Lowry, *Number the Stars.* Boston: Houghton Mifflin, 1989, p. 137.

6. Franklin Delano Roosevelt, "Four Freedoms Speech." www.nelson.com.

7. Glendon, *A World Made New,* p. 10.

8. United Nations, "Charter of the United Nations," June 26, 1945. www.un.org.

9. Quoted in Glendon, *A World Made New,* p. 24.

10. Quoted in Glendon, *A World Made New,* p. 151.

11. Quoted in Glendon, *A World Made New,* p. 151.

12. United Nations, "Universal Declaration of Human Rights," preamble.

13. United Nations, "Universal Declaration of Human Rights," art. 2.

14. United Nations, "Universal Declaration of Human Rights," art. 4.

15. United Nations, "Universal Declaration of Human Rights," art. 9.

16. United Nations, "Universal Declaration of Human Rights," art. 14.

17. Quoted in Glendon, *A World Made New,* p. 48.

18. United Nations, "Universal Declaration of Human Rights," art. 28.

19. United Nations, "Universal Declaration of Human Rights," art. 1.

20. William F. Schulz, *In Our Own Best Interest.* Boston: Beacon Press, 2001, from the foreword by Mary Robinson, p. ix.

Chapter 2: Government Brutality

21. Quoted in Digital Freedom Network, "'I Will Pay with My Life': Salvador Allende's Last Speech," February 18, 1999. www.dfn.org.

22. Marc Cooper, "Twenty-Five Years After Allende," *Nation,* March 23, 1998. http://past.thenation.com.

23. Pamela Constable and Arturo Valenzuela, *A Nation of Enemies: Chile Under Pinochet.* New York: W.W. Norton and Company, 1991, p. 20.

24. Quoted in Robinson Rojas Sandford, *The Murder of Allende and the End of the Chilean Way to Socialism.* New York: Harper and Row, 1976, p. 203.

25. John Conroy, *Unspeakable Acts, Ordinary People.* New York: Knopf, 2000, p. 170.

26. Quoted in Kerry Kennedy Cuomo, *Speak Truth to Power: Human Rights Defenders Who Are Changing Our World.* New York: Crown Publishers, 2000, pp. 49–50.

27. Conroy, *Unspeakable Acts, Ordinary People,* p. 6.

28. Steven Lee Myers, "Word for Word/U.S. Army Training Manuals," *New York Times,* October 6, 1996, sec. 4, p. 7.

29. Sir Nigel Rodley, "Report on Torture and Other Cruel, Inhuman or Degrading Treatment or Punishment," United Nations General Assembly, Fifty-Fourth Session, A/54/426, October 1, 1999, part 5, item 60.

30. Amnesty International, "China: Amnesty International Welcomes Release of Tibet's Longest Serving Prisoner of Conscience," news release issued by the International Secretariat of Amnesty International, ASA 17/016/2002, April 4, 2002.

31. Quoted in Cuomo, *Speak Truth to Power,* p. 249.

32. United Nations, *The United Nations and Human Rights: 1945–1995.* New York: United Nations Department of Public Information, 1995, p. 151.

33. Quoted in Shaharyar M. Khan, *The Shallow Graves of Rwanda.* London: I. B. Tauris, 2001, pp. 16–17.

34. Khan, *The Shallow Graves of Rwanda,* from the foreword by Mary Robinson, p. vii.

Chapter 3: The Rights of People at Work

35. Quoted in National Labor Committee, "Testimony: Zenayda Torres, Chentex Factory, Las Mercedes Free Trade Zone/Managua, Nicaragua," September 2000. http://nlcnet.org.

36. Quoted in National Labor Committee, "Testimony."

37. Quoted in National Labor Committee, "Testimony."

38. Quoted in Ginger Thompson, "At Home, Mexico Mistreats Its Migrant Farmhands," *New York Times,* May 6, 2001, p. 1.

39. International Labour Organization, "Social and Labour Issues in Small-Scale Mines," sec. 2, May 1999. www.ilo.org.

40. International Labour Organization, "Social and Labour Issues in Small-Scale Mines," sec. 3.

41. Eric Brazil, "Official Salvadoran Report Says Its Factories Are Brutal," *San Francisco Chronicle,* May 11, 2001, p. A16.

42. Barry Bearak, "Lives Held Cheap in Bangladesh Sweatshops," *New York Times,* April 15, 2001, p. 1.

43. Robert B. Reich, "American Sweatshops," *American Prospect Online,* January 18, 2001. www.prospect.org.

44. United Students Against Sweatshops, "Who We Are." www.usasnet.org.

45. World Bank, "New World Bank Report Urges Broader Approach to Reducing Poverty," press release no. 2001/042/S, September 12, 2000. http://wbln0018.worldbank.org.

46. International Labour Organization, "Your Voice at Work," International Labour Conference, Eighty-Eighth Session, 2000. www.ilo.org.

47. Quoted in NACLA, "The Gap and Sweatshop Labor in El Salvador," *Report on the Americas,* January–February 1996, p. 37.

48. Quoted in Tony Evans, ed., *Human Rights Fifty Years On: A Reappraisal.* Manchester, England: Manchester University Press, 1998, p. 163.

Chapter 4: Women's Rights Are Human Rights

49. United Nations, "Universal Declaration of Human Rights," art. 2.

50. United Nations, *The United Nations and Human Rights,* p. 450.

51. Quoted in Rebecca J. Cook, ed., *Human Rights of Women.* Philadelphia: University of Pennsylvania Press, 1994, p. ix.

52. United Nations, "Women's Rights Are Human Rights," Spring 2000, from the foreword by Mary Robinson. www.unhchr. ch/html/menu2/womenpub2000.htm.

53. Quoted in Claudia Dreifus, "A Conversation with Nawal Nour: A Life Devoted to Stopping the Suffering of Mutilation," *New York Times,* July 11, 2000, p. F7.

54. Quoted in Dreifus, "A Conversation with Nawal Nour," p. F7.

55. Quoted in Pratibha Parmar and Alice Walker, "Warrior Marks," New York: Harcourt Brace and Company, 1993, pp. 256–257.

56. Quoted in Parmar and Walker, "Warrior Marks," p. 259.

57. Quoted in Parmar and Walker, "Warrior Marks," pp. 292–293.

58. United Nations, "Women's Rights Are Human Rights."

59. U.S. Department of State, "Trafficking in Women and Children: The U.S. and International Response," Congressional Research Service Report 98-649 C, May 10, 2000. http://usinfo.state.gov.

60. Quoted in Human Rights Watch, "Owed Justice: Thai Women Trafficked into Debt Bondage in Japan," part 4: Profiles, September 2000. www.hrw.org.

61. Quoted in Human Rights Watch, "Owed Justice."

62. Amnesty International, "Saudi Arabia: Time Is Long Overdue to Address Women's Rights," news service no. 181, September 27, 2000. http://web.amnesty.org.

63. Quoted in Amnesty International, "Saudi Arabia."

64. United Nations, "Women's Rights Are Human Rights."

Chapter 5: Strategies to Promote Human Rights

65. Schulz, *In Our Own Best Interest,* from the foreword by Mary Robinson, pp. ix–x.

66. Quoted in Cuomo, *Speak Truth to Power,* p. 57.

67. Quoted in Cuomo, *Speak Truth to Power,* p. 178.

68. Quoted in Cuomo, *Speak Truth to Power,* p. 236.

69. Quoted in Marguerite Guzman Bouvard, *Women Reshaping Human Rights.* Wilmington, DE: Scholarly Resources, 1996, p. 233.

70. Quoted in Jonathan Power, *Like Water on Stone: The Story of Amnesty International.* Boston: Northeastern University Press, 2001, p. 17.

71. Oxfam International, website homepage. www.oxfam.org.

72. U.S. Congress, *Anti-Apartheid Act of 1986,* 99th Congress, H.R. 4868. http://thomas.loc.gov.

73. Robert F. Drinan, *The Mobilization of Shame.* New Haven, CT: Yale University Press, 2001, p. 183.

74. *Oxfam International,* "Debt Relief: Still Failing the Poor," April 2001, p. 2.

75. Oxfam America, "Debt Relief: Essential to Poverty Relief," 2001. www.oxfamamerica.org.

76. World Bank, "Financial Impact of the HIPC Initiative: First Twenty-Five Country Cases," HIPC Unit, March 2002, p. 5. www.worldbank.org.

77. Quoted in Richard Chacon, "4 US Errors in Guatemala Cited; Admits US Backed Military Regimes," *Boston Globe,* March 11, 1999, p. A1.

78. Schulz, *In Our Own Best Interest,* p. 140.

79. Quoted in Middle East Watch, *Human Rights in Iraq.* New Haven, CT: Yale University Press, Human Rights Watch Books, 1990, p. 110.

80. Quoted in Cuomo, *Speak Truth to Power,* p. 67.

Organizations
to Contact

Amnesty International
322 Eighth Ave.
New York, NY 10001
(212) 807-8400
website: www.amnesty.org

Founded in England in the 1960s, Amnesty International today has close to 1 million members and offices in dozens of
countries. Amnesty is most famous for its letter-writing campaigns on behalf of political prisoners, but its activities go far
beyond such campaigns. Amnesty observes and reports on
human rights violations in every corner of the world and lob-
bies on behalf of human rights, often presenting its findings
to the United Nations. Its website offers brief press releases
and in-depth reports on virtually every human rights issue
imaginable.

Food Research and Action Center (FRAC)
1875 Connecticut Ave. NW, Suite 540
Washington, DC 20009
(202) 986-2200
website: www.frac.org

FRAC is a nonprofit, nonpartisan public-policy center seeking
to reduce hunger in the United States. FRAC conducts research
on hunger and serves as a watchdog in Washington, D.C.,
monitoring government policies that affect hunger. FRAC also
supports local and national groups that work to assure Ameri-
cans have access to food.

Human Rights Watch

350 Fifth Ave., 34th Floor
New York, NY 10118
(212) 290-4700
website: www.hrw.org

Based in New York, Human Rights Watch investigates and reports on human rights abuses worldwide. Its website is well organized and easy to navigate, offering a vast amount of up-to-date information and superbly written reports on international human rights concerns.

International Labour Organization (ILO)

4, Route des Morillons CH-1211
Geneva 22 Switzerland
(41)-(22)-799-6111
Washington, DC Branch Office: (202) 653-7652
website: www.ilo.org

Founded in 1919, the ILO is a United Nations specialized agency dedicated to furthering social justice and internationally recognized human and labor rights. Many international conventions and agreements on issues of labor have been brokered by the ILO, which includes more than 170 countries as members.

MADRE

121 W. 27th St., Room 301
New York, NY 10001
(212) 627-0444
website: www.madre.org

A human rights organization focusing on women's rights, MADRE works with grassroots human rights groups to address issues of health, education, and economic development, among other rights. MADRE was originally founded to work on issues in Nicaragua and still maintains a close connection to Central America, although its work has broadened to embrace international concerns.

National Labor Committee (NLC)
275 Seventh Ave., 15th Floor
New York, NY 10001
(212) 242-3002
website: www.nlcnet.org

Founded in 1981, the National Labor Committee devotes itself to the human rights of workers, including the struggle to better conditions in the clothing industry. The NLC has organized campaigns around the baseball manufacturing industry in Haiti and garment manufacturers in Central America, among other labor issues.

Oxfam America
26 West St.
Boston, MA 02111
(617) 482-1211
website: www.oxfamamerica.org

Oxfam America is a nongovernmental organization (NGO) connected to a group of eleven similar organizations worldwide, which together comprise Oxfam International. The Oxfams work to end poverty and promote economic and social human rights, lobbying governments, coordinating humanitarian aid, and working on economic development programs worldwide.

United Nations (UN)
UN Public Inquiries Unit, Room GA-57
New York, NY 10017
(212) 963-4475
website: www.un.org

The United Nations was founded in 1945 to guarantee international security and promote human rights worldwide, among other raisons d'être. The United Nations has sponsored numerous international human rights agreements, including the original Universal Declaration of Human Rights, available on its website at www.un.org/Overview/rights.html. The United Nations is connected to a family of organizations, including the UN Children's Fund (UNICEF) and the UN Development Programme (UNDP). In 2000–2001, the budget of the UN was more than 2.5 billion dollars. Presently, its membership includes 189 countries.

The World Bank
1818 H St. NW
Washington, DC 20433
(202) 477-1234
website: www.worldbank.org

One of the world's largest sources of development assistance, the World Bank was created after World War II as part of a group of international economic institutions focused on rebuilding Europe. The World Bank today has economic ties to more than 100 countries. Its website is an excellent source for statistics and information on international economic development and poverty.

Suggestions for Further Reading

Kerry Kennedy Cuomo, *Speak Truth to Power: Human Rights Defenders Who Are Changing Our World.* New York: Crown Publishers, 2000. A superb collection of interviews with human rights activists from all over the world. The activists included in this collection work on issues as diverse as child labor, political representation, the human rights of gays and lesbians, and police brutality.

Mary Ann Glendon, *A World Made New: Eleanor Roosevelt and the Universal Declaration of Human Rights.* New York: Random House, 2001. A fascinating account of the drafting of the Universal Declaration of Human Rights, with a particular focus on the role of Eleanor Roosevelt.

Myra H. Immell, ed., *Ethnic Violence.* San Diego, CA: Greenhaven Press, 2000. Contains essays and articles on ethnic violence, including the genocides in Armenia, Rwanda, and Yugoslavia. Racial violence within the United States is also addressed.

Susan Kuklin, *Iqbal Masih and the Crusaders Against Child Slavery.* New York: Henry Holt and Company, 1998. An informative account of the young human rights activist Iqbal Masih, who spoke out against child labor in his home country of Pakistan. Masih was assassinated at the age of twelve.

Works Consulted

Books

Marguerite Guzman Bouvard, *Women Reshaping Human Rights.* Wilmington, DE: Scholarly Resources, 1996. A collection of writings by and biographies of women human rights activists.

John Conroy, *Unspeakable Acts, Ordinary People.* New York: Knopf, 2000. A book exploring the dynamics of torture from both the point of view of those who have tortured others and the point of view of the victims of torture.

Pamela Constable and Arturo Valenzuela, *A Nation of Enemies: Chile Under Pinochet.* New York: W.W. Norton and Company, 1991. A history of Augusto Pinochet's rule in Chile, written by a *Boston Globe* journalist and a professor of government at Georgetown University.

Rebecca J. Cook, ed., *Human Rights of Women.* Philadelphia: University of Pennsylvania Press, 1994. A collection of essays reflecting on the tradition of human rights and how it relates to the lives of women around the world.

Robert F. Drinan, *The Mobilization of Shame.* New Haven, CT: Yale University Press, 2001. A recent book on human rights by Jesuit priest and Georgetown University law professor Robert Drinan.

Tony Evans, ed., *Human Rights Fifty Years On: A Reappraisal.* Manchester, England: Manchester University Press, 1998. A collection of essays examining the state of international human rights fifty years after the adoption of the Universal Declaration of Human Rights.

Richard A. Falk, *Human Rights Horizons.* New York: Routledge, 2000. An academic book by Princeton human rights scholar

Richard Falk looking at the state of human rights today and considering current strategies for promoting human rights worldwide.

Shaháryar M. Khan, *The Shallow Graves of Rwanda.* London: I.B. Tauris, 2001. An account of the days following the genocide in Rwanda, as told by the UN Secretary General's Special Representative in Rwanda.

Lois Lowry, *Number the Stars.* Boston: Houghton Mifflin, 1989. A young adult novel about two Danish girls during World War II, as one flees to Sweden to escape the Nazi persecution of the Jews.

Martha Meijer, ed., *Dealing with Human Rights.* Bloomfield, CT: Kumarian Press, 2001. An eclectic collection of essays about human rights as it relates to Asia.

Middle East Watch, *Human Rights in Iraq.* New Haven, CT: Yale University Press, Human Rights Watch Books, 1990. A report from the human rights organization Human Rights Watch on rights violations in Iraq. This book evaluates U.S. policy toward Iraq through the 1980s. It was published shortly before the U.S. war with Iraq.

Kate Millett, *The Politics of Cruelty.* New York: W.W. Norton and Company, 1994. An intriguing look at the dynamics of torture, written by feminist scholar, activist, and writer Kate Millett.

Johannes Morsink, *The Universal Declaration of Human Rights: Origins, Drafting and Intent.* Philadelphia: University of Pennsylvania Press, 1999. An excellent account of the drafting of the Universal Declaration of Human Rights, with an emphasis on the types of rights included in that document and the reasons certain rights were included.

Pratibha Parmar and Alice Walker, *Warrior Marks.* New York: Harcourt, Brace and Company, 1993. A look at the issue of female genital mutilation, including interviews with women's rights activists in Africa who struggle against the practice.

Jonathan Power, *Like Water on Stone: The Story of Amnesty International.* Boston: Northeastern University Press, 2001. A history of the human rights group Amnesty International, with chapters discussing human rights issues in Guatemala, Nigeria, and other places around the world.

Nina Redman and Lucille Whalen, *Human Rights: A Reference Handbook,* 2d ed. Santa Barbara, CA: ABC-CLIO, 1998. An excellent reference book on human rights, including the texts of major UN human rights agreements.

Robinson Rojas Sandford, *The Murder of Allende and the End of the Chilean Way to Socialism.* New York: Harper and Row, 1976. The harrowing story of General Pinochet's coup d'état in Chile, told shortly after the event.

William F. Schulz, *In Our Own Best Interest.* Boston: Beacon Press, 2001. The executive director of Amnesty International USA argues in this book that there are practical reasons— beyond ethical ones—for citizens of the United States to promote human rights at home and abroad.

United Nations, *The United Nations and Human Rights: 1945–1995.* New York: United Nations Department of Public Information, 1995. A compilation of UN human rights documents.

Periodicals

Amnesty International, "China: Amnesty International Welcomes Release of Tibet's Longest Serving Prisoner of Conscience," News Release issued by the International Secretariat of Amnesty International, ASA 17/016/2002, April 4, 2002.

Barry Bearak, "Lives Held Cheap in Bangladesh Sweatshops," *New York Times,* April 15, 2001.

Eric Brazil, "Official Salvadoran Report Says Its Factories Are Brutal," *San Francisco Chronicle,* May 11, 2001.

Richard Chacon, "4 US Errors in Guatemala Cited; Admits US Backed Military Regimes," *Boston Globe,* March 11, 1999, p. A1.

Timothy Connor, "We Are Not Machines," Sponsored by Clean Clothes Campaign, Global Exchange, Maquila Solidarity Network, Oxfam Canada, and Oxfam Community Aid Abroad, March 2002.

Claudia Dreifus, "A Conversation with Nawal Nour: A Life Devoted to Stopping the Suffering of Mutilation," *New York Times,* July 11, 2000.

William Echikson, "It's Europe's Turn to Sweat About Sweatshops," *Business Week,* July 19, 1999.

Steven Lee Myers, "Word for Word/U.S. Army Training Manuals," *New York Times,* October 6, 1996.

NACLA, "The Gap and Sweatshop Labor in El Salvador," Report on the Americas, January–February 1996.

Oxfam International, "Debt Relief: Still Failing the Poor," April 2001.

Sir Nigel Rodley, "Report on Torture and Other Cruel, Inhuman or Degrading Treatment or Punishment," United Nations General Assembly, Fifty-Fourth Session, A/54/426, October 1, 1999.

Ginger Thompson, "At Home, Mexico Mistreats Its Migrant Farmhands," *New York Times,* May 6, 2001.

United Nations, "Press Conference on International Day for Victims of Torture," press briefing, June 25, 1999.

Washington Post, "How to Battle Sweatshops," February 2, 2001.

Internet Sources

Amnesty International, "Saudi Arabia: Time Is Long Overdue to Address Women's Rights," news service no. 181, September 27, 2000. http://web.amnesty.org.

Gunnar Berge, "Presentation Speech: 2001 Nobel Peace Prize," December 10, 2001. www.nobel.se/peace/laureates/2001/presentationspeech.html.

Marc Cooper, "Twenty-Five Years After Allende," *Nation,* March 23, 1998. http://past.thenation.com.

Digital Freedom Network, "'I Will Pay with My Life': Salvador Allende's Last Speech," February 18, 1999. www.dfn.org.

Human Rights Watch, "Owed Justice: Thai Women Trafficked into Debt Bondage in Japan," part 4: Profiles, September 2000. www.hrw.org.

———, "World Report 2002: Events of 2001, November 2000–November 2001." www.hrw.org.

International Labour Organization, "Social and Labour Issues in Small-Scale Mines," May 1999. www.ilo.org.

———, "UN Secretary General Emphasizes Global Compact's Importance," July 26, 2000. www.ilo.org.

———, "Your Voice at Work," International Labour Conference, Eighty-Eighth Session, 2000. www.ilo.org.

National Labor Committee, "Testimony: Zenayda Torres, Chentex Factory, Las Mercedes Free Trade Zone/Managua, Nicaragua," September 2000. http://nlcnet.org.

———, "Toys of Misery: A Report on the Toy Industry in China," January 2002. www.nlcnet.org.

Oxfam America, "Debt Relief: Essential to Poverty Relief," 2001. www.oxfamamerica.org.

Oxfam International, website homepage. www.oxfam.org.

Robert B. Reich, "American Sweatshops," *American Prospect Online,* January 18, 2001. www.prospect.org.

Franklin Delano Roosevelt, "Four Freedoms Speech," January 6, 1941. www.nelson.com. Audio excerpts can be found at http://usinfo.state.gov.

United Nations, "Charter of the United Nations," June 26, 1945. www.un.org.

———, "Fact Sheet No. Twenty-Three: Harmful Traditional Practices Affecting the Health of Women and Children," Office of the High Commissioner for Human Rights. www.unhchr.ch/html/menu6/2/fs23.htm.

———, "Universal Declaration of Human Rights," December 10, 1948. www.un.org.

———, "Women's Rights Are Human Rights," Spring 2000. www.unhchr.ch/html/menu2/womenpub2000.htm.

U.S. Congress, "Anti-Apartheid Act of 1986," 99th Congress, H.R. 4868, October 2, 1986. http://thomas.loc.gov.

U.S. Department of State, "Trafficking in Women and Children: The U.S. and International Response," Congressional Research Service Report 98-649 C, May 10, 2000. http://usinfo.state.gov.

United Students Against Sweatshops, "Who We Are." www.usasnet.org.

World Bank, "Financial Impact of the HIPC Initiative: First Twenty-Five Country Cases," HIPC Unit, March 2002. www.worldbank.org.

————, "New World Bank Report Urges Broader Approach to Reducing Poverty," press release no. 2001/042/S, September 12, 2000. http://wbln0018.worldbank.org.

Index

Picture Credits

About the Author

Keith McGowan has taught high school, coordinated an elementary after-school program, and worked as a business researcher for New York Times Digital. He has lived in Australia, Chile, and Haiti, and he has traveled extensively through east Asia, including China and Laos. He is currently planning a trip through India. He is the author of two previous Lucent books: *Sexual Harassment* and *Hazardous Waste.* He lives in Massachusetts.

MOSAIC I
A Content-Based Writing Book